Calypso's Secrets

Isabelle Kane

Published by
Satin Romance
An Imprint of Melange Books, LLC
White Bear Lake, MN 55110
www.satinromance.com

This story is dedicated to Andy, Aslan, Charlotte, and Johan with all my love.

WHAT THEY ARE SAYING ABOUT
CALYPSO'S SECRETS

"CALYPSO'S SECRETS by Isabelle Kane is an engaging story that has all the necessary elements for a great intrigue. Fabulous characters, a gorgeous setting, and a riveting tale that will keep you hooked until the end. I know this novel will delight all who read it!" - Nadine St. Denis of Romance Junkies

"For a wonderful diversion, I invite you to pull up a comfortable chair and delve into the pages of CALYPSO'S SECRET. It's an exciting and fast paced read just right for these lazy spring days." - Diana Risso of Romance Reviews Today

"Isabelle Kane has crafted a solid romantic suspense that is sure to delight fans. From beginning to end, readers are treated to a story that somehow manages to keep some of its secrets hidden until the very end... So if you are looking for a romantic suspense that will get your blood pumping, grab yourself a copy and start reading." - Amanda of Fallen Angel Reviews

Chapter One

Skylar Connelly juggled a bottle of Diet Coke, her keys, her purse, a bag of chips, and a sack of grape Big League Chew Bubble gum. Why hadn't she taken the bag the cashier in the run-down, overstocked, little gas station had offered her?

Trapping her purchases up against the car door, she freed her hand and managed to fit the key into the lock and turn it. In doing so, she dropped the diet Coke bottle, and it hit the ground and rolled about.

"Great."

She set her purse and merchandise on the hood of her ancient, navy blue Golf, and picked up her soda. As she straightened, her gaze caught on the photo of the smiling blond girl, which stood propped up by the gear stick.

Determinedly she swallowed the lump in her throat. She had to keep it together, for Maia's sake.

It was definitely turning out to be one of those days. She shoved some sweaty, damp tendrils back from her face and jerked the car door open. As she sat down on the hot vinyl car seat, she heard a car pull up behind her, but ignored it and picked up the picture. It had been taken last summer, here, in the Florida Keys. Maia looked so carefree, freckled, and happy smiling at her from the deck of some yacht.

Skylar couldn't ignore the revving of a powerful engine behind her. The person back there could just wait a minute. She needed a few seconds to pull herself together.

Her gaze was irresistibly drawn back to the shot of her sister. Maia was wearing a halter-top and shorts, and sitting next to a very solemn boy of about ten. He wasn't smiling for the camera. He held up his hand as if to fend the sun away, while Maia squinted her green eyes right at the camera. Nothing had ever fazed her, not even the heat and sunshine of a tropical summer.

The car behind her honked its horn. Skylar glanced in her rear-view mirror. A gaudy, bright yellow Jeep with heavily tinted windows was right behind her. She guessed a tint that dark was illegal—she couldn't see the driver at all.

The car door opened. A tall, blond man with a broad-shouldered, linebacker's build was unfolding himself from the driver's side.

As he walked toward her door, he looked disgustingly cool, comfortable, and in his element in his khaki slacks and white dress shirt.

"Damn." She reached for the key and shoved it into the ignition. She had no desire to be the victim of a road rage incident.

"Come on, Bessy." She turned the key. The engine cranked and caught, spewing diesel exhaust out, and into the face of the man who was now just behind her car. Popping the Golf into gear, she puttered away. Bessy backfired just as the old car turned back onto the main road.

Glancing in the mirror, she saw the man had removed his sunglasses and was wiping at his face.

Skylar felt a moment's regret there was nothing worse than getting a mouth full of diesel exhaust. "Probably a jerk," she muttered to herself as she pulled back onto US1.

Needing to get her mind off Maia, she turned the radio on. Flipping through the stations, she found she couldn't find a song she liked. She needed a real pick me up. She needed...*Elvis!*

It was an inspired choice. Rifling through her cassette carrier and glancing between it and the road, she eventually located the tape she wanted and shoved it into the cassette player.

Soon, she was rocking along with Elvis. She kept the rhythm by tapping on the steering wheel, trying to block out the fact the air blowing on her face was hot and humid.

She peered out through the bug guts, already beginning to adorn the windshield she'd just squeegeed off at the gas station. There it was, the famous Seven Mile Bridge. It, and its predecessor, arched over the aqua-green water like white rainbows. As Skylar bopped along, she glimpsed fisherman scattered here and there along the old bridge. Both bridges

2

were really impressive engineering feats, and they meant she was moving in on her destination, Coral Key.

Elvis was now crooning about fools rushing in, and she wasn't even half of a mile up on the bridge when she happened to glance in her rearview mirror. A familiar yellow Jeep was rapidly bearing down on her.

"Shoot."

In very short order, the Jeep was crowding her bumper.

"Are you insane?" She watched the other car in her rearview mirror, feeling decidedly anxious with the Jeep right up behind her on the bridge. She gestured with her arm for the driver to pass.

The Jeep accelerated smoothly into the other lane. When the two cars were parallel, the driver lowered his passenger side window, so he could look right at her. He tilted his sunglasses down and waved as he slid on by. Once he was clear of Bessy, he cut in front of her. His vanity license plate read: "CPT STUD."

Captain Stud honked and sped away.

"Neanderthal."

The guy had definitely ruined the view from the Seven Mile Bridge for her.

To her dismay, crossing the bridge didn't indicate she was close to her destination. An hour passed as she drove from island to island, past the Key's bizarre mixture of huge mansions, rinky-dink motels, and surf shops. The islands were tropically exquisite, but with something of the touristy feel of the Jersey shore.

The heat seemed to be increasing with each passing moment. Skylar cursed her own stupidity in not dressing more appropriately for the weather. She should have worn shorts, but she had opted to look professional and sophisticated. Now, she guessed she just looked rumpled, flushed, and worn out. She was debating pulling over and calling to verify her route when she saw the sign, Welcome to Coral Key.

On this island, the honky-tonk abruptly ceased. On both sides of the road, she saw only lush greenery and attractive fences that blended well with the surroundings. She glimpsed jewel–like blue beyond the roofline of one magnificent mansion. Clearly, this was a high-rent district.

"Okay, *330 Pelican Cove Drive*…here it is." She took a sharp right, and proceeded along a massive stucco wall running parallel with the road. Another right had her facing an immense wrought iron gate. The number *330* was worked into the curlicues of iron.

"This is it, Bessy." She patted her steering wheel and peered through the gate. Her heart was beginning to pound anxiously. "What now?"

"Please advance your vehicle to the white line and state your business." A disembodied voice rang out.

"Wha-What? Hello? Where are you?"

"Please speak into the intercom."

"Where is it?"

"Advance to the white line. The intercom will be to your immediate left."

"Um...Oh, I see it now."

"What is your name?"

"Skylar Connelly...I'm expected. I'm the new swimming instructor for Mr. Escalle's nephew."

"Your name is on the list. Proceed into the parking lot at the rear of the house. Park your vehicle in one of the staff carports. Have a good day."

The wrought iron gates slowly and majestically began to open in. Once they were wide, she followed the driveway. A magnificent Spanish-style stucco mansion with red roof tiles and shutters and creamy white walls came into view.

Skylar paused, taking it all in. The wrought iron of the gate was incorporated into the house design on the various balconies and in fanciful detail work. The house was recessed back into a sheltering cove of pine, palm, and Poinciana trees. The landscaping had a romantic, lush feel to it, and revealed the hand of a master gardener in the layout of the flowerbeds, ornamental shrubs and trees, and energetically climbing vines.

There was a lower wall of the same style as the exterior wall that enclosed a courtyard at the front of the house. Through the twin arches, she could make out red paving, an abundance of terra cotta potted plants, and an elaborate water fountain.

Abruptly, she realized she was gawking. She took her foot off

Bessy's brake, and eased around the side of the mansion. She came upon a blacktopped parking lot that was shadowed and just dappled with the light that penetrated through the overhanging canopy of trees. There were several open parking slots.

The driveway continued out toward the water where an impressive yacht glistened whitely in the Florida sunshine. She glimpsed three men moving about at work on board the vessel.

To her immense dismay, an outrageously bright yellow jeep was backed up to the dock. It couldn't be.

That would be just her kind of luck. After all, what were the odds?

There was no point in worrying about it. She drove headfirst into one of the parking slots, and tucked Maia's picture under the passenger side seat. It would be too dangerous to bring it in with her. She climbed out, and had just popped the trunk on Bessy, when she caught sight of a disturbingly familiar tall blond man, now wearing flip flops, cut off jeans, and a salmon pink T-shirt, headed her way.

The T-shirt advertised "Mr. Zogs Sex Wax," and bore the legend "the best for your stick."

Chapter Two

It was Captain Stud. Her nemesis from the gas station. Now, he looked comfortable, disreputable, and distinctly sexy from his broad chest, to the lean, chiseled, hairy legs. How could he have changed so fast? She hadn't been going slowly when he'd passed her.

Having no choice but to brazen it out, Skylar drew her purse strap over her shoulder, shoved her makeup case under an arm, and grabbed a suitcase in one hand and her duffle bag in the other.

"Need some help, sweet thing?"

As he stepped out from beneath the shadows of the overarching palm trees, she nearly ground her teeth at the patronizing offer.

"Couldn't resist following me, could you?" He shoved his sunglasses back onto his head, revealing a tan, rugged, but boyishly handsome face with warm, golden brown eyes. She guessed he was in his late twenties or early thirties because of the fine laugh lines bracketing his lips and the creasing at the corners of his eyes.

"Don't be absurd. I had absolutely no idea we were going to the same place. I thought you were some kind of speed junky with a death wish."

"Babe, you're the road hazard. You were going about forty in a fifty-five."

"I let you pass me."

"Playing games like that on the road could get you into serious trouble some day. You're lucky I'm a forgiving kind of guy."

"Yes, well, I suppose it's best if we simply forget about the episode."

"Honey, I said I would forgive you, not I would forget about it.

Here, let me take your bag. You're carrying more than enough weight with that chip on your shoulder." He reached for her body-sized duffle bag.

In reaction, she jerked her arm back. "Here, if you want to help me, take this." She nearly flung her suitcase and her make-up case at him. There was no way she was going to relinquish the duffle bag, not with her thirty-eight revolver hidden inside it.

He didn't comment on her over-reaction. He simply leaned down and picked up the suitcase. As he did so, she caught a whiff of his fresh and zesty cologne. The man had the easy summer gracefulness of a surfer, but there was no lazy carelessness in those assessing eyes.

"Do I make you nervous, doll?"

"I don't appreciate being referred to by such misogynistic nicknames." Skylar was chagrined at how prissy she sounded.

"How's 'doll' misogynistic?"

"It's extremely demeaning and chauvinistic. My name is Skylar Connelly."

"I'm Luke White."

"Do you work here?"

"Yeah. I'm sort of Mr. Escalle's man Friday. Can you manage okay? I'll take you over to the house. Lillian has been waiting for you all afternoon."

"I don't think I'm late," she muttered as she glanced down at her watch. "I said I would get here sometime this afternoon. It's a little after four, so I'm not late."

"Relax, Skylar. She's just looking forward to meeting you."

He led her through an archway into a courtyard at the back of the house. It was smaller than the front courtyard, and decorated with blooming potted flowers, and comfortable lounge chairs. A Spanish style wrought iron door led from this area into a sort of utility room. From here, they proceeded up a long corridor.

Skylar peeked through opened doorways and decorative arches to catch glimpses of luxurious rooms decorated in a modern, tropical style in a palette of sea greens, corals, and lush ivories. The deep pile cream carpet beneath their feet muffled their footsteps.

"Lil-lian," he called, once they were in an immense open room. On

7

both sides, sweeping staircases curved their way up to the second floor. An enormous oriental carpet, which repeated the themes of ivory, pale pink and light green covered the pale rose Italian marble floor.

The room was sparely furnished but exquisite in the overall impact of its architecture and its furniture. There were two inlaid, antique wooden buffet pieces placed on either side of the archway through which they entered. A matching gold and white sofa, which looked distinctly uncomfortable, and a pair of mint green chairs formed a seating arrangement along one wall. The stiff, formal elegance left Skylar feeling grubby, disheveled, and rather plebeian.

Enormous beveled windows flooded the room with late afternoon sunlight. There were no personal touches to the room except for a pair of portraits, one on either wall about half way up each staircase. One was of a darkly elegant man with a lean face, and black hair with just a touch of silver to it. He was a very handsome man, in an aging Antonio Banderas sort of way. He was posed beside an armchair in a study, and he was staring out of the picture in such a way he almost appeared to be watching Skylar.

She stifled the juvenile impulse to take a step in each direction to see if those dark eyes would follow her.

The other portrait was of a young woman whose dark hair and eyes revealed she was related to the man. She, too, was attractive, thin, and expensive looking. She was dressed to the nines in a sparkling evening ensemble, but there was a discontented curve to the woman's full lips that Skylar found unsettling.

"Lillian. The new nanny is here."

"I am not a nanny."

"Okay," Luke cocked one thick, blond eyebrow at her. "The child care professional has arrived."

"You're impossible." She smothered a smile.

"I just thought you were angling for the politically correct term."

"I'm coming, Luke," rang out from somewhere upstairs.

"Welcome to Casa del Mar." A woman who spoke with a decided southern accent appeared at the top of one staircase. She wore her silvering blond hair up on her head in a French twist, and a light, summery dress sort of floated around her as she descended.

As she came toward her, Skylar realized this was a big woman, at least six feet tall and solidly built. Nonetheless, she had a fluttery, butterfly-like air to her that somehow diminished her stature so she seemed petite and delicate.

The lady held out both hands in greeting. "It's wonderful you made it. I'm Lillian. I know Martin will be thrilled when he finds out you are here." Before Skylar could draw back, or react, Lillian air-kissed her by one cheek and then by the other.

"Hello. I'm Skylar Connelly." Never comfortable with touchy-feely greetings from strangers, she took a step backwards. She was from the Northeast. You didn't air-kiss in New Hampshire.

"You poor thing. You look worn out. Are you thirsty or hungry? What can I get you?"

"I'm fine. I grabbed a sandwich at a Cuban deli on Largo."

"I'm sure you could use some of my sweet tea. I'll go and get you some. Luke, would you be a dear and take Ms. Connelly up to her room?"

"Please call me Skylar."

"And you must call me Lillian."

"Where is she staying?" Luke picked up her suitcase.

Lillian clapped her hands together. "Luke White, what are you wearing? What is this young lady going to think of you? You look so handsome in a button down shirt and a respectable pair of slacks."

"Now, Lillian, I know you would be disappointed if I showed up wearing my Sunday-going-to-meeting duds."

"You are a devil, Luke. What am I going to do with you?" She wagged her finger at him with a fond smile. "I've put Skylar in the Dolphin Suite."

"Dolphin Suite?"

"The blue suite near Christopher's rooms." To Skylar, she said, "I thought it would be more comfortable for both you and the boy than your sleeping in the servants' area. Consuela, Chris's nanny, has her room just on the opposite side of the same hall. Luke, the door is open. I'll be up in one minute. I just want to get the sweet tea."

Once Lillian had hurried away, though Skylar wasn't sure *hurried* was quite the right word, the woman sort of glided, quickly, Skylar glanced over at Luke. "Lead the way."

"I like a submissive woman."

"Don't you ever quit?"

"That's what all my lady friends ask, not that they're complaining."

They were halfway up the steps when she inquired, "Dolphin Suite?"

He grinned. "Lillian redecorated this house last year. Each bedroom has a theme. I'm in the guesthouse. She calls my bedroom Mediterranean Magic."

Despite herself, Skylar chuckled as she followed him down another long but more narrow hallway. They passed several closed doors, which she guessed led into bedrooms.

"Here we are." He kicked the door wide with his foot. "The kid's room is just down the hall." He set her suitcase down.

The room was aptly named. The bed was draped in diaphanous blue. Matching curtains had been drawn back from French doors, which led onto a balcony. The curtains were held by cunning gold dolphins. The furnishings, including a lovely vanity and dresser, were a light, airy, white French provincial.

"This is my room?" She was frankly surprised. She hadn't expected such luxury for a mere swim coach.

"Yup. Here, give me your purse."

Without thinking, she simply passed over the large, leather bag.

He unzipped it, and peered inside. He rummaged through and pulled things out. First, came her checkbook, then her hairbrush, followed by her calendar.

"What are you doing?" She was outraged and reached to grab the bag.

"I told you I'm in charge of security here. I didn't carry your bags up here to play bellhop."

"You can't just...That's my private property."

"I'm under orders from the boss." Ignoring her efforts, he turned his back to her. His long arms and broad shoulders effectively boxed her out.

"You have no right..." she began.

"If you have a complaint, take it up with the boss, or quit. It doesn't really matter to me. I'm just doing my job... Why do women have to carry everything but the kitchen sink with them? This thing has to weigh thirty pounds." With this observation, he raised it up and unceremoniously dumped the contents out onto the silky, pale blue comforter.

"Whoa, what's this? A Beretta. I'm impressed." He glanced over at her. "There's something really hot about a chick who packs heat. Do you know how to use it? Lookee here, pepper spray, and a knife, too."

"It's a diving knife."

"I'd guess the pepper spray is for the sharks. What are you so worried about? This is Coral Key, not New York City."

"I live alone. I have to look out for myself."

Luke eyed her skeptically as he expertly removed the bullets from the handgun. He casually stuffed them into his pocket. "I bet no one messes with you. I thought you were from New Hampshire."

"I am."

"New Hampshire really must have changed since I was last there."

"I live in D.C. now."

"I'll have to confiscate these." He patted his pocket with one hand, and held up the gun with his other. "I'll let you keep the rest." He indicated the pepper spray and the diving knife. "I'll see you at dinner, babe."

"Look, I'm not a 'babe'. I find that term disrespectful."

"Would you prefer 'sweet cheeks?'"

She shook her head despairingly. "Aren't you going to go through my other bags?"

"Oh, I'll come back and search the room when you're unpacked."

"You're serious?" She was incredulous.

"Martin is serious about security, even when it comes to babysitters with pretty green eyes."

He sauntered from the room.

As he closed the bedroom door, she sat down on the bed. "Stupid. Stupid." Luke was probably reporting her suspicious behavior at this very moment. The man was maddening, but also clever and witty. She would have to be very cautious around him. She doubted he missed much.

It was too bad she had to meet him under these circumstances—she admitted to herself, he was exactly the sort of sexy, irreverent, athletic man she found most attractive.

She glanced at her diving bag. The snub-nosed thirty-eight revolver her mother had given her was still buried in the foot of one of her flippers. She looked around the room. Where to hide it? There was nowhere safe where it would be handy.

She decided to leave it where it was for right now. She would lock the bag in her car at the earliest opportunity, that was, unless Mr. Escalle told her to take her stuff and get out that very night.

"Knock-knock," Lillian called from the doorway. She was carrying a tray with a clear glass pitcher filled with rich, brown tea and two tall, ice-filled glasses. She set her burden down, and after filling the glasses, held one out to Skylar.

"Thank you."

"I've been looking forward to having you here. I hope you like to chat. I have so missed having nice, long talks with my lady friends since we have been here in the Keys."

"Are you…I mean, are we the only women here?"

"Oh, no, not at all." She sat down in one chair, and Skylar took the one opposite her.

"There are several other women here at Casa del Mar, it's a pretty name, don't you think, if not very original. There's Yvette, but she and I don't have much in common, and Angelique, but she has been traveling quite a lot lately. Consuela is just not a gossipy soul. I've always been an advocate of the more the merrier. It makes for much more interesting dinner conversation. Don't you agree?"

"Yes. Sure. My mother feels the same way. Can you tell me something about Christopher?" She wanted to learn all she could about the child who was the reason for Maia's and her own employment on Coral Key. In addition, this was the sort of question Lillian probably expected her to ask. Skylar fully intended to cultivate a friendship with the older woman. Perhaps doing so could help her in her search for her sister.

Lillian crossed her ankles demurely in the classic debutante position. Her hands rested quietly on her lap, until she spoke, when they became animated. "Chris is a dear boy, but so sad, so quiet, and so fearful. Ever since his father died he…well, he hasn't been the same. Mr. Hollins, his tutor has been wonderful with him."

"He has a tutor?"

"Mr. Hollins has him in the mornings, for his lessons, and you will have him in the afternoons. Consuela, she goes by Connie, has him for meals and in the evenings. Do you have any other questions, dear?"

She had many questions. The first one that came to mind was an obvious one. *Do you know anything about my sister Maia's disappearance?*

Then again, she couldn't ask it and expect to remain on the premises.

"The ad I answered asked for a college caliber swimming coach who had experience with children. I don't mean to be intrusive, and I'm very glad Mr. Escalle was so selective, but why didn't he just enroll his nephew in some swimming lessons at a YMCA or any other athletic club? Is he a very…um…protective uncle?"

"Well, my dear, it's rather complicated. You will soon see Mr. Escalle only hires the best. For example, Mr. Hollins is working on his PhD in Classical Studies. There is another issue here as well. You see, Chris is terrified of water. There was a family tragedy…But this is neither the time nor the place to get into…Oh, dear, here I am talking your ear off, and you look just tuckered out…Do you like the sweet tea?"

"It's delicious." Actually, Skylar had been too fascinated to take even a sip. Now she hurriedly swallowed some of the icy cold sweetness. It was rich, sugary, and revitalizing.

"It's my grandmother's recipe."

"It's really good…Lillian, what sort of business is Mr. Escalle in?"

"He's very diversified. He's into importing and exporting anything from coffee beans to bananas. He also owns real estate. He has his finger in lots of pies."

The housekeeper said, "Now, you tell me about yourself."

"Well, I'm working on my Master's in Kinesiology, you know, Physical Education. I also coach swimming at Haverhill College. I needed to take some time to work on my thesis, and I've always wanted to see the Florida Keys. This seemed like the perfect working vacation."

"The Keys are lovely, even though they are getting so touristy and tacky. Papa Hemingway must be spinning in his grave. There are so many homosexuals down here now. Why it's just like San Francisco."

Skylar barely managed to keep from rolling her eyes. One of her closest friends from her Olympic days was a lesbian, and Skylar had no patience with prejudice. Still, she could see no upside on attacking the older woman on the point. She needed to get along with her, for Maia's sake.

"That fellow who carried my bags. I'm terrible with names…"

"You mean Luke." Lillian grinned fondly.

"He's quite a character. What does he do here?"

"Luke is *bon vivant* and a scoundrel, but he makes my old heart go pitter-patter. He does all sorts of things for Mr. Escalle." She waved a hand expansively. "But his real interest," here Lillian leaned forward secretively, her voice became confiding, "his real interest is in treasure hunting."

"He's a treasure hunter?"

"Yes, dear, a treasure hunter, *a la* Mel Fisher. Mel Fisher," Lillian repeated catching her puzzled look. "He searched for decades in the waters off the Keys for sunken Spanish galleons. Finally, miraculously, he discovered one and she was filled with gold. Her name was the *Anoka*. Are you at all familiar with the story? No? Well, Fisher and his family set up a museum detailing the whole adventure in Key West. You'll have to visit it.

"Luke is the captain of Mr. Escalle's yacht, the *Calypso*, and a diver, but treasure hunting is his real passion," she smiled fondly. "Luke is a charmer. If I were twenty years younger…" She added as an afterthought, "Also, he handles security for Mr. Escalle's family when they stay here at Casa del Mar. Mr. Escalle really enjoys himself down here. He doesn't have all sorts of bodyguards around him, the way he has to in Miami. We maintain a light staff here. I like it this way, too."

So, the laid back, too handsome surfer was, indeed, head of security at Casa del Mar. Skylar had the unsettling feeling that, despite his demeanor, he missed little.

"You manage the household?"

Lillian nodded.

"Luke said you decorated this room. You are very talented." Skylar

14

glanced around the lovely room, taking in the dolphin figurines and accessories which were subtly incorporated throughout. Maia always loved dolphins. Had she stayed in this same suite?

"Thank you, dear. Actually, I redid all of the bedrooms last year. They were rather dated, and some of the curtain fabrics had faded. I am pleased with the results. If you'd like, I can give you the grand tour tomorrow. You probably want to settle in a little right now."

"Sounds good. I would enjoy seeing the rest of the house. It's such a showplace." Skylar smiled. The tour would provide her with an opportunity to get the layout of the house before she started searching for clues to Maia's disappearance.

"I do hope you like seafood."

"Yes, I do."

"Thank goodness. We tend to emphasize seafood while here in the Keys, of course. I'll see you later, at dinner. We dine at seven." She patted Skylar's hand as she passed by on her way to the bedroom door.

Skylar stood up. "Lillian, would it be all right if I walked around a little? On the beach, I mean."

"Oh yes, of course." She glanced at Skylar's apparel critically. "We do dress for dinner, dear. Nothing too formal, but casual-chic."

"All right. Thanks."

The older woman left the room, discreetly closing the door behind her.

Skylar unzipped one side of her battered suitcase and rummaged around. She pulled out a wrap around mini-skirt, a pale yellow tee-shirt, and a pair of sandals. After she'd changed, she French braided her hair back. Just before leaving the room, she hefted her diving bag, which still contained the thirty-eight, onto her shoulder and took one last look around. If Luke searched the bedroom, he would find nothing suspicious.

She headed back the way she'd come, through the grand room with the twin staircases, and encountered no one as she went all the way back to the car port. There, she unlocked Bessy and put the bag in the back. She unzipped the bag, and dug around until her fingers encountered the cold stock of the handgun. She shoved it deeper into the bag, and then relocked the car.

With her luck, Luke was probably skilled at breaking into cars. She could just imagine those long, tanned fingers skillfully manipulating a tool...

Whoa. She stopped herself. She had to stay focused. For Maia's sake, she couldn't allow lust for Luke White to cloud her thinking.

Chapter Three

With a sense of relief, Skylar followed a path strewn with tan bark, which led to the beach. The air was heady with the scent of blooming Poinciana trees. Tropical flowers flourished side by side with more delicate northern varieties. She passed by two gardeners who were tending the colorful flowerbeds.

"Hello."

Both glanced up at her, and nodded greetings.

The gardens were enclosed by a stucco wall, which separated them from the sand. She opened a gate through an elaborate wrought iron trellis about which a lush green vine hung. Then, she was on the beach.

The beach was vacation brochure perfect with quietly lapping emerald water and soft sand. The view was also magnificent. In the distance, she could make out palm trees on another island.

It was a windy day, and the curls around her face danced in the breeze. She bent down and removed her sandals. She wanted to dig her toes into the sand. She stepped out into the water, and allowed the cool liquid to lap at her tired feet and calves. The afternoon sun was decadently warm on her shoulders. Skylar felt worlds removed from the cold, gray, northern climate she left just two days before. She took a deep breath. For a moment, she allowed the serenity of the scene to ease her worries about Maia.

She meandered slowly down the beach, passing other properties. She kept walking for more than a half-an-hour because the beach was open and unfenced, unlike the grounds of the houses along it. The afternoon sunlight matured, became more golden and rich. She wondered what time it was, and decided to head back.

17

It soon became apparent she'd walked farther than she'd intended. Where was the house?

She began to walk rather quickly. Then, she glimpsed a flash of color in the sky, and she held a hand up to shield her eyes. It was an elaborate emerald and scarlet dragon kite. A small boy was holding onto the kite as it danced wildly high up in the sky. A tall, thin man stood near him.

Skylar waved her arms. "Hello!"

Both of them turned to face her. The man bent and spoke to the boy, then walked towards her. Just then, she glimpsed the vine-covered trellis that led into Casa del Mar.

Thank goodness. She'd found her way back.

The boy hung back. Could this be Christopher? She guessed the man with him was the tutor whom she'd been told about, the classics scholar. He appeared to be in his early twenties, a few years younger than Skylar, closer to her sister's age. He was way too young to be her employer.

"Hi, I'm Skylar Connelly. I was lost, but now I know where I am. That's Casa del Mar there, and that would make this young man Chris Whitfield, right?"

Chris didn't move.

The tutor stepped forward. A few inches taller than her five-feet ten-inches, he was tan from the Florida sun and had large, deep set eyes. He wore his brown hair, which was already slightly recessed from his forehead, militarily short, and was dressed very Northeast, in his white golf shirt, creased khaki shorts, and deck shoes. He glanced over her, pausing for a moment to glare at the frosted blue polish on her toenails.

She resisted the urge to curl her toes into the sand.

"Have we met?" His accent was upper class Boston.

"Not yet, but Lillian told me about you."

"Why on earth would she do that?"

She was taken aback by the hostility. "We're going to be working together. You see…"

"What do you mean 'working together,'" the thin lips sneered.

"If you'd let me finish." Why had Maia liked this place? Granted, the climate was nice, but, in Skylar's opinion, with the possible exception of Lillian, the inmates at Casa del Mar were definitely on the weird side. "I'm here to work with Chris. I'm to teach him to swim and the basics of some other sports. Look, Lillian told me your name. I just can't remember it. Help me out here."

The suspicion faded from his eyes. He extended one lean hand. "Forgive me…I thought you were one of Mr. Escalle's…friends. Please, call me Cole. I knew a Physical Education person was coming. It's just I pictured you somewhat differently, older, larger, more masculine, more like the PE teachers I had as a child."

Now his expressive features shifted into a friendly and very open smile. "If I had had a PE teacher who looked like you, I might not have feigned illness so often." The smile revealed very even, orthodontically-enhanced, white teeth. The expression in the brown eyes was flirtatious.

"You were a PE dropout?" Skylar queried with a smile.

"I was driven to it by the three-hundred-pound, sadistic Neanderthal who taught it at the prep school I attended."

"Cole, I would appreciate an introduction to this young man."

"Yes, of course."

The boy didn't move as they neared him. He didn't even glance at them, just stared more determinedly at his dragon dancing high up in the sky. He was tall for his age, thin, and wore a surprisingly stern expression, and his dark eyes were distant and unwelcoming.

He was a pale child, and neither his skin nor his hair showed he'd lived in South Florida for all of his eight years. Still, he would have been a pretty child, if his expression were friendlier. Skylar felt as though the eyes of a grownup were gazing up at her from the diminutive face.

"Hello, Chris. I'm Skylar."

Now the kid stared at her, but said nothing.

She squatted down so their eyes were on a level. "You're doing a really nice job with that kite. I like flying kites, too. We're going to have lots of fun this summer. We'll play soccer and basketball. Have some fun in the water."

Chris shook his head. "No, I won't."

Great. So much for having a way with children. If Luke didn't get her fired for packing heat, Cole would for her failure to get along with Chris.

"It'll be a blast. We'll go snorkeling along the coral reef. We'll swim…"

"No! I won't! He can't make me." With that, Chris broke away, releasing the kite as he took off running toward the house, his arms pumping furiously with his efforts. The dragon kite bobbed wildly high up in the air, but the string and the handle were already out of reach over the ocean.

"What was that all about?"

"No one warned you?"

"Warned me about what? I was hired to work on the boy's swimming."

"Who interviewed you?" Cole queried. "I know it's none of my business, I'm just curious."

"An attorney named Bill Thompson. I met with him in October."

"Usually, Thompson is very thorough. I'm surprised he didn't better prepare you for the challenge you're facing."

"What do you mean?"

"Chris saw his father drown. Mr. Escalle took the family out on his yacht to celebrate Chris's fifth birthday. Jim Whitfield had had a few too many cocktails and fell overboard. Since the accident, Chris has been abjectly terrified of water."

"Oh, jeez. I feel like an idiot." She contemplated how devastating it must have been for the boy to witness his father's death.

"It's not your fault. You should have been warned. Martin believes Chris has to conquer his fear. He even makes Chris go out on the yacht, but the child won't leave his stateroom. I've heard him crying… Apparently, you are to be the solution to all of these problems.

"To be honest, Skylar, I am opposed to forcing the water issue with Chris. He doesn't need to be traumatized further. Now that I've met you, I can only hope you will try to be sensitive to what the boy has been through. Now, if you will excuse me, I have to change for dinner. I'll see you there?"

"Oh, yes. Thanks for explaining the situation to me."

"I hope you understand I don't take issue with you specifically."

"I understand, and we'll just take it one day at a time. I won't force Chris to do anything he is uncomfortable with. Rest assured."

Cole nodded, but looked dubious. Then, he turned and followed the boy's footprints back toward the house.

Left alone to consider the beauty of the impending sunset, Skylar stared at the orange and pink streaks beginning to appear along the horizon line.

Learning about Chris's father's death made her feel a kinship with the boy. She, too, understood the anguish of suddenly losing a loved one, but she refused to believe Maia was irrevocably gone. She came to Coral Key to find answers and to find her sister.

"Maia, Maia, why did you stay here? This is such a strange place."

On the other hand, Maia had always been committed to making a difference with her life. In college, she had been working toward a double major in Social Work and Elementary Education. She must have felt Chris needed her.

"Maia, I hope I don't let you down. I don't even know where or how to start looking for you."

Skylar trudged slowly back toward the house. As she made her way up the steps in the enormous room she'd dubbed the 'ballroom', she heard the murmur of voices against a backdrop of classical music coming from somewhere past the archway and down the hall. A woman laughed. Clearly, the people of the house were congregating.

Once in her room, she decided she didn't want to appear too casual for her first meeting with Escalle, even though it might prove to be her last, if Luke decided to make problems for her. She rifled through her suitcase and pulled out a long, loose sundress made of a wrinkly, dark blue fabric, which clung to her long lines and curves. It had the advantage of not needing to be ironed.

She quickly changed and then checked her appearance in the vanity mirror. Her long, dark hair was now riotously curling because of the humidity, so she twisted it up onto her head, and shoved pins into place, securing it, but left the smaller corkscrew tendrils to frame her face.

She put her contact lenses in, but couldn't force herself to do much as far as makeup was concerned. Her skin was relishing the warm, moist air far too much to abuse it with cosmetics. After she put on just a little mascara and lip-gloss, she was done. Leaving her room, she followed the sound of voices down the stairs, along the hall, and into a sunken great room. There, several people were gathered.

The first thing she noticed was the huge windows showcasing sky and water. Scarlet streaks were all that remained of the sunset, and the sea around Casa del Mar was blood red with reflected brilliance. The *Calypso* gently rocked at dock. The fading sunset painted it, too, blood red.

The view was so amazing, so breathtaking, Skylar was momentarily lost in it. A low wolf whistle from right by her ear called her back to herself. She turned to find Luke White standing right behind her.

Involuntarily, she took a step back, and then regretted having done so.

"My, my, we were hiding our light under a barrel, weren't we?"

Luke appeared somewhat more respectable now. He was wearing beige slacks, and a faded, turquoise-blue, button down shirt. His sun-streaked blond hair was still damp from the shower and brushed back from his face. He had shaved, and Skylar was immediately aware of the scent of his darkly sensual cologne. Like a pheromone, it entered her system and suggested mindless pleasure.

He grinned at her.

Chapter Four

"Mr. White," Skylar edged her words with ice, hoping to throw some cold water on the warm burn in his eyes.

"It's Luke, sweetheart." He took her hand and raised it to his lips. "You look good enough to eat."

She jerked away "Mr. White," she began, intending to deliver a scathing remark.

"Luke, you have to introduce us to your new friend." A woman's voice broke in. The dark-haired woman whose portrait hung in the entrance hall smiled archly at her.

Skylar stepped away from Luke.

Angelique Whitfield was very pretty, but with a hard, sharp edge to her appearance. She was very tanned and thin to the point of gauntness, except for her surgically enhanced breasts and collagen-puffed lips. She was in her late thirties, and dressed expensively. Her face was expertly made up. She was smiling at her, but her brown eyes remained distant.

"You must be Chris's mother. He definitely has your eyes." Skylar offered the other woman her hand. Angelique stared at it, then slowly took it.

Skylar found the smaller woman's grip surprisingly firm.

"Yes, I'm Angelique." The woman had the sort of perfectly toned, petite body, which made her feel giant-like and awkward in comparison.

"I met Chris on the beach this afternoon. The resemblance between you is remarkable."

For a moment, Angelique's hard expression softened. "Thank you, but I think Chris looks more like his father."

"Now, now, Angelique," a cultured tenor voice chimed in. "Everyone remarks Christopher," the boy's full name was carefully enunciated, "is all you. The Escalle genes run true. And you, lovely lady must be the newest addition to our little household. Skylar Connelly, I am Martin Escalle."

From her research, Skylar knew her new employer was in his late forties, but the skin on his lean, aquiline features was suspiciously taut and smooth. Cynically, she wondered if he had had a face-lift. His eyes and hair were dark, though there was the slightest hint of distinguished gray at his temples. More than the glossy presentation, there was a strong resemblance between brother and sister, despite the more than ten-year age difference between the two. Neither was extremely beautiful, but both were striking, thin, and well packaged.

Skylar shook his hand. "Hello, Mr. Escalle. I'm very glad to be here."

"Welcome to my home. Let me introduce you to the rest of our little party." He took her arm. "You have met Luke and Angelique, and this is Yvette."

"Hello."

The other woman didn't move from her languid position on the couch. She merely inclined her head in acknowledgement. "*Bon jour.*"

Yvette was exquisite, young and perfectly proportioned from her endlessly long, cellulose-free legs and waist to her overly bountiful breasts. Her eyes were a shocking silvery-gray shade, and her straight, platinum hair framed the exotic perfection of her features. She was wearing a very short, very diaphanous dress that revealed more than it concealed. She sipped on something clear, turning away, making it plain she had no interest in Skylar.

"I'm sure you have already met Lillian," Escalle said. "As you will soon learn, she makes everything run smoothly here at Casa del Mar. If you have any questions or need anything at all, she is the lady to ask."

Lillian appeared like a partridge next to a peacock seated beside the flamboyant Yvette. The housekeeper was wearing a dress Skylar guessed her mother would describe as 'tastefully conservative' and her blond hair was drawn back from her face in a French twist. The older woman preened at the praise and smiled warmly at Skylar.

"My dear," Lillian announced. "I wanted to introduce you to a very bright young scholar with whom you will be collaborating, but he appears to be running late."

Just then, Skylar heard footsteps in the hallway. Cole appeared in the doorway.

"Ah, here he is. This is Cole Hollins. Skylar Connelly."

"I hope you weren't waiting for me. Skylar and I met on the beach."

Her employer glanced at her.

"I was walking on the beach. It's been so long since I've been in such a lovely, warm climate."

"Each day here is as lovely as the day before and the day after," Escalle stated. "I have lived in many places, and I believe the Florida Keys have the best climate, bar none, in the months of December through March…Luke, please get Skylar something to drink."

"What would you like, Miz Connelly?" He mockingly drawled.

"Just a Diet Coke would be fine."

"You can't drink Diet Coke your first night in the Keys. Let me surprise you."

"I really would just prefer…"

"Luke is a really talented 'mixologist,'" Lillian offered. "It'll do you some good. You had quite a drive today."

"All right then, whatever." She decided not to ruffle any feathers.

"That's the spirit," Lillian applauded.

"I'm going to raid the refrigerator," Luke said. "I need some of Rene's ingredients."

"Now don't you bother him, Luke," Lillian admonished. "You know how he gets at supper time."

"Mr. Escalle…Mr. Escalle, you have a phone call." A swarthy, muscle-bound fellow announced from the doorway.

"I'll be right there, Bill. If you will excuse me, this should take but a minute. If Rene is ready before I get back, just go ahead and start without me."

"We'll wait for you, Martin," Angelique said.

As Escalle walked to the doorway, Bill looked Skylar up and down and offered her a leering grin.

She felt an immediate, visceral dislike for the man.

"Here you are." Luke reappeared in the other doorway.

He handed her a large goblet filled with frothy, white iciness, his gaze meeting hers over the glass. He held onto the goblet for a few seconds more than was necessary, his eye contact, steady and challenging.

She wondered what his game was. He obviously hadn't told Escalle about finding her gun. She couldn't imagine Escalle keeping her around after such a discovery, or at the very least demanding an explanation, particularly, if, as she suspected, there were suspicious or even illegal goings on occurring at Casa del Mar. If one of these people did something to Maia, she knew this person wouldn't hesitate to dispose of her in similar fashion.

"It's a margarita," she observed as she sunk down into one of the chairs.

"Not just any margarita, but my specialty."

She sipped at the concoction hesitantly. "This is really good. I mean, I haven't had many margaritas to compare it with, but this is delicious."

Luke moved to lounge in a chair opposite her. "Sweetheart, what can I tell you, I'm good."

"Modest, too." She couldn't resist the slight barb. The guy just got under her skin.

"Hey, I believe in calling a spade a spade, but then, you aren't straight forward are you, Miz Connelly?"

"Have you two met before?" Angelique questioned.

"No... Well, Luke did pass me on the Seven Mile Bridge."

"Oh, it's just you two seem so...familiar with each other."

"We've never met before today."

"No, there's no history between us, just chemistry."

Skylar choked in the middle of a sip of her margarita.

Luke moved quickly and thumped her soundly between the shoulder blades.

"Thanks," she glared at him as she recovered.

He grinned at her audaciously.

Angelique eyed them both suspiciously.

"Dinner should be quite a treat." Lillian sought to ease the tension in the room. "Rene is making *Pompano en Papillote*. It's one of his specialties."

"It sounds delicious," Skylar agreed, though she had no clue what this entrée entailed.

"Tell us something about yourself." Angelique was focused intently on Skylar. "What sort of qualifications do you have to work with my son?"

"Please, Angelique," Escalle remonstrated as he reentered the room. "I assure you Miss Connelly is eminently qualified to work with Christopher. I am hurt you would question my judgment with regard to my nephew."

"It's not that I don't trust you, Martin. I just want to know more about the people who will be working with Chris…I worry about him."

"You have enough to busy yourself with planning that luncheon for the manatees."

"It's for the Key deer, Martin."

"I love fresh venison," Yvette purred.

"Don't be stupid, Yvette," Angelique snapped. "Those deer are an endangered species."

"My sister is very involved in environmental causes." Martin explained with a smile Skylar could only describe as patronizing.

"Do you realize how much of the Key deer's habitat is destroyed each year?" Angelique asked Escalle.

"I have no idea. Nor am I interested, but I will do my bit for the little fellows. Just let me know how much to make the check out for and to whom. As for Chris' education, rest assured I will make the appropriate decisions."

Skylar watched the exchange with interest. Though she found the older woman pushy, she felt sorry for her now. Escalle obviously had total control where Chris was concerned, even though Angelique didn't seem like a disinterested mother. Now, she was nibbling at her collagen filled lower lip. It was obviously a nervous sort of reaction, which betrayed her dissatisfaction with her brother's edict.

Skylar decided to throw her a bone. "Mrs. Whitfield, I'm a certified lifeguard and a licensed physical education teacher. I'm working on my Master's degree at Haverhill College where I'm also the assistant swimming coach. Please go ahead and ask me any questions you have."

"Were you fired or let go from your former position? I thought swimming was a winter sport. Did you leave mid-season?"

"I took the semester off to complete my thesis. Though my doing so will probably make the rest of the season more demanding for my fellow coaches, I did give them two terms of advance notice. They know I have to complete my Master's degree soon in order to stay employed. With teaching and coaching, there simply wasn't enough time to work on my thesis. Since we didn't have much talent on the team this year, it was definitely the time to do it."

"Do you have any experience with children?"

"I've worked with children every summer for the past few years. While in college, I taught at the YMCA. I taught in and now oversee Haverhill's summer swimming instructional program for kids of all ages, from six months to mid-teens. If you'd like to see it, I can print you out a copy of my resumé."

"Do those credentials satisfy you?" Escalle chided his sister.

"I'm sorry, Martin. Chris is a very sensitive boy, and you know how he is about the water."

"This is the right thing to do, my dear. Trust me. Don't I always know what's best for you and for Christopher?"

"You're right." Angelique offered her brother a weak smile. Then, she took a more than delicate swig of her cocktail. The tigress defending her young was gone now. Her brother had effectively and completely undermined her.

"Is Chris dining with us this evening?" Skylar asked.

"Not tonight. He ate earlier with Consuela, his nanny."

"Dinner is served," announced a maid in full black and white uniform.

Angelique and Lillian led the way into the dining room. Skylar scooted forward to get up. Yvette stepped in front of her, blocking her from rising. To Skylar's surprise, she didn't apologize. She just smirked as she passed by.

"I see you and Yvette are already hitting it off," Luke murmured as he offered her his arm.

* * * *

Skylar set her alarm for six-thirty. The golden Florida sunshine was already piercing the sheer, blue bed drapings when it woke her up. Resisting the urge to close her eyes and steal a few more minutes of sleep, she tossed back the covers and rose determinedly to her feet. She was to join Chris for breakfast. Before that, however, she intended to get in a morning swim in the ocean.

She often did her best thinking in the water, and she wanted to refocus on her quest to find out what happened to Maia. She also needed to work through the unsettling affect Luke had on her. As she drove herself through the water, she considered the disturbing possibility this man, to whom she was undeniably attracted, may have been involved in her sister's disappearance.

After her swim, she joined Lillian, Chris, and a stout, middle-aged lady with a kindly face for breakfast in the round, airy breakfast chamber, which had a bay window overlooking a small walled garden.

"We're so pleased you could join us, Skylar. Aren't you all rosy-cheeked? How was your swim?"

Skylar blinked as she took a seat next to the boy, who refused to meet her eyes. "The water was great." How did Lillian know about her swim?

"Luke is a great one for swimming as well. He also enjoys snorkeling and scuba diving. Maybe you two could swim together. Then, I wouldn't worry about either of you. I just don't think it's a good idea to swim alone."

"It's very kind of you, but I don't think Luke would be too keen on the idea. He and I just don't seem to get along very well." She planned to keep as much distance as possible between them.

"That surprises me. After you retired last night, he asked Mr. Escalle all sorts of questions about you. He seemed intrigued by you."

Skylar sought to ignore the fluttering in her stomach. So much for working out her attraction to him. With her comment, Lillian had managed to evoke all of her confused thoughts and feelings with respect to Luke White.

"Chris, this is Miss Connelly. She's going to be your new athletics instructor." Lillian beamed fondly at the boy who was angrily stabbing his fork into his French toast.

"Hi, Chris. You can call me Skylar."

He studiously ignored her.

"I'm Conny," the other lady offered with a pleasant smile. "I'm Chris's nanny. You've already been out swimming? How very motivated of you. My Carl tells me it's best to get one's exercise done early in the morning, but I have a hard enough time just getting out of bed. I'm simply

29

no good until I've had my morning coffee." Conny was plump, matronly, and sent off warm, fuzzy vibes. "Do you have something special planned for Chris today?"

Chris announced, "I'm not swimming. You can't make me swim."

"Chris," Conny said. "That's no way to speak to Skylar. Let's use our royal manners. You apologize."

"No. I'm not. I don't like her."

"I'm not going to make you do anything," Skylar countered. "How do you feel about a game of tennis? Then, I thought we could play a little hide-and-seek in the gardens."

"Chris," Conny beseeched. "Give Skylar a chance. You're always complaining because I won't play outside with you."

"You're not gonna trick me," he asserted as he glared at her. "I won't swim. You can't make me."

"Chris, I promise you we won't go near the water today. I give you my word."

He studied her skeptically. "Well…I guess I don't mind tennis much."

"Good. Let's go and get changed."

He would get some exercise, and she would have the opportunity to get a better sense of the layout of the property. A game of hide-and-seek would provide a plausible explanation for nosing around, looking for clues that would explain what happened to her sister at Casa del Mar.

Twenty minutes later, the two of them were hitting balls back and forth over the net on the professional quality court behind the house. Surprisingly, the kid was reasonably athletic and not a bad tennis player, but he didn't try very hard. He wouldn't chase after balls he probably could have gotten, and he was in poor physical condition. Still, she believed in teaching through positive reinforcement.

"You're pretty good," she shouted. "You've taken some lessons, haven't you?"

"Yeah, so?"

"What's your favorite sport?"

"Golf's okay, and basketball, but I can't shoot very well."

"I could teach you how to shoot."

"Girls don't know how to shoot."

"Oh, I don't know. I'm actually pretty decent. I bet I could give you some pointers. You could really impress the other guys at your new school."

He studied her for a moment. "You think so?"

"I know so... Your serve. What other things do you like to do, Chris?"

"I like computer games... Oof," he grunted as he volleyed the ball back.

"You about ready for a water break?"

"You said no water."

"Water to drink."

"Yeah, okay." The boy was red-faced and sweating as he took a seat on the bench under an enormous Poinciana tree beside the court.

She passed him a water bottle and a towel. "Who do you play tennis with around here?"

"Mr. Hollins plays with me sometimes, and Luke does, too, when he's not too busy. He's looking for treasure, you know."

He sounded excited for once, so she decided to play along. "Is he?"

"There's like a whole bunch of old-time Spanish boats sunk around the Keys. Luke's gonna find one of them one day. They're supposed to be full of gold and jewels and other cool stuff."

Skylar refrained from rolling her eyes. At least the kid was enthusiastic about someone. To this point, she hadn't seen him display enthusiasm about anyone or anything, including herself.

"He takes the yacht out every day, and he scuba dives looking for clues and stuff. Uncle has all this special equipment on the boat for him. It's awesome."

Out of the mouths of babes...It was possible the boy had inadvertently given her two critical keys to the mystery of Maia's disappearance. It seemed likely Luke and Escalle were working together in a scheme that utilized the Calypso. What was Luke doing out on the yacht every day? All sorts of possibilities, few of them legal, entered her mind. Was he importing drugs, gun running, or smuggling something else? At least now she had a lead to pursue. She glanced back at Chris. The boy had also just given her some leverage on himself.

"Would you like to help Luke one day?"

"Yeah, but I'm just a kid."

"You could certainly go out with him on your uncle's yacht, and he could teach you to use some of the equipment. Why I know lots of kids your age who can snorkel."

Chris was quiet for a moment. "I don't like going out on the boat." He beat his tennis racket against his shoes.

Skylar realized she'd pushed too far, too fast. He had been severely traumatized by his father's death. It wasn't fair or kind to try manipulate him with his hero worship of Luke. She felt somewhat chagrined by her own behavior. She decided to change tactics. "Mel Fisher. He was a treasure hunter, wasn't he? I think I saw a Discovery channel special on him. Didn't he build a museum down here?"

"Oh yeah. It's filled with treasures, like gold coins and bars. There's a video that shows how he looked for like the longest time until he found the *Anoka.* That's the name of the ship."

"Would you like to go to the museum?"

"I've been there once, but I want to go again."

"I'll take you there on Friday if you do something for me."

"What?"

"I want you to work with me in the pool for half an hour each day."

"No way." The kid stood up.

"Look, Chris. I know you're scared, but your uncle hired me to teach you how to swim. If I fail, he'll probably hire someone else, someone tougher and meaner. I'm willing to go slowly. You set the pace. Your uncle is not going to give up until you're swimming. If you don't deal with your fear this winter, you'll definitely have to at your boarding school. So, it's your choice, now, and we take it easy and go slowly, or later, and you hope the coach at your school is sympathetic and won't embarrass you in front of the other boys."

"I don't want to do it! I won't. You can't make me."

"You're right about that, but give me a chance. Give me a week. At the end of the week, I'll take you to the Mel Fisher museum regardless of how our lessons are going. If you're still unhappy about swimming, then after the week, I'll quit. Now come on, what have you got to lose?"

"You'd really quit cause I told you to?"

"You have my word."

"We'll stay in the shallow end, and you won't make me do anything I don't want to?"

"I promise."

He took a deep breath. "Okay." He walked slowly and heavily back to his side of the court. Once there, he angrily wiped at his cheeks. "You're right. He'll make me do it sometime."

Skylar didn't like pressuring Chris. It was important for him to learn to swim with living near the ocean as he did, but she had the sense the boy would benefit from some therapy as well. He'd suffered a major trauma, and he harbored real resentment for his uncle, not even referring to him by name. The two were clearly at odds.

The fact Escalle was trying to force his damaged, fragile nephew to do something he was terrified of suggested Escalle's smooth, in-charge manner masked a ruthless will. She wondered how and if Maia had run afoul of him.

The rest of the day passed smoothly and uneventfully. Skylar enjoyed a delicious lunch with Chris, Lillian, and Conny. Then, Lillian gave her a tour of the house. Afterwards, she hurried to her room to make a rough map of the layout. She also wanted to get into the guesthouse where Luke stayed. She imagined it wouldn't be difficult to convince Lillian to show off more of her interior design work. It might prove more challenging to get onto the yacht. She would have to work on that one.

She had the afternoon free as Chris worked on his academic lessons with Cole. She spent it walking around the grounds. The entire perimeter was fenced, and she was disturbed to find surveillance cameras at every entrance gate.

In her meanderings, she passed several thuggish-looking men who were either on their way into the house, presumably to see Escalle, or out to the yacht, to see Luke. All in all, Casa del Mar was a very strange and suspicious place.

Why hadn't Maia been more honest about her job in her e-mails? She had said it was a beautiful place and the pay was great. It was only in her later missives she mentioned her suspicions something illegal was taking place at the mansion by the sea. Why hadn't Maia just left? Skylar suspected Chris and her sister's tender heart were the reasons she stayed on. She hadn't wanted to worry Skylar or their mother, so it had only been when matters really got out of hand that she related her concerns.

"Please, God, let Maia be okay. Please." Skylar was following in her sister's footsteps, though it was becoming increasingly clear they led somewhere perilous.

* * * *

"Count to twenty this time. Then come find me." Chris shouted gleefully as he took off.

"Stay out of your Uncle's study," Lillian admonished sternly.

"Just hide in one of the main rooms, okay?" Skylar obediently closed her eyes and counted out loud. Despite the fact he was eight years old, Chris loved hide-and-seek and wanted to play it almost every day. He was very good at it, and both the grounds and the house offered excellent hiding opportunities. Skylar didn't mind playing because each game provided her with a reasonable excuse for snooping around.

All in all, things were going rather well, at least superficially. The swimming lessons were progressing slowly. On that very morning, she'd gotten Chris to stand waist deep in the water. The poor kid had been abjectly terrified, trembling with fear, but he'd been game. She was proud of him.

Unfortunately, as yet she'd discovered nothing about the circumstances surrounding Maia's disappearance.

"Eighteen. Nineteen. Twenty. Ready or not, here I come."

"You two do seem to be hitting it off," Lillian observed as she sipped her sweet tea.

"He's a nice boy." Skylar stood up. "Oh yes, Lillian, I almost forgot. I wanted to ask you if you know of any children Chris' age around here. It would be really good for him to play with other kids."

Connie spoke up, "My nephew lives over on Ramrod Key. His son, Tyler, is a year younger than Chris. I could bring him here some afternoons after school. I'm just not sure Mrs. Whitfield would approve."

"Why wouldn't she approve?"

"She's rather overprotective of Chris."

"There's no harm in asking. As long as you don't mind, I will."

"I'd love to see more of Tyler. No, go right ahead, ask away. You'd best go looking for the boy. I think I heard him go up the stairs. I'd look in the black Japanese cabinet in the upstairs hallway."

"Thanks."

"Chris, here I come," Skylar sang out as she jogged down the hall. "When I find you, I'm going to tickle you." She heard light, running footsteps overhead. "I hear you."

As she took the stairs two at a time, she heard a door shut and hurried in the general direction. She found herself on a different corridor than the one on which her own room was located. At the end of this hall, there were three doors, one, in front of her, and one on either side of her. She tried to recall what rooms these were from Lillian's tour and the map in her bedroom, but then, she reconsidered. She was better off playing dumb if she was found looking around. After all, the house was huge. She couldn't be expected to remember which room was which based on a quick tour.

"I'm coming, Chris."

Her heart was beating rapidly. She reached for the knob and turned it. "Come on, Chris. You know I said bedrooms were off limits. You better not be in here." She spoke loudly for the benefit of anyone other than Chris who might be listening. She pushed the door open. The room was bright as the curtains had been drawn back from a pair of large windows. It was done in tan with burgundy accents. The dark, mahogany furniture was heavy and impressive and looked antique. Old English foxhunting prints adorned the walls. It was clear Lillian had been going for a Victorian look in this bedroom. But there was an impersonal feel to the room marking it as a guest room.

The closet door had been left opened. So, Skylar peeked inside. She found men's clothing meticulously organized and separated into shirts and slacks, formal and informal. Shorts were even hung.

On the dresser, she saw a set of keys, a comb, cologne, hair spray, and a heavy, silver watch. A pile of papers was stacked on the desk by the closed laptop computer. She glanced at the top page and glimpsed the words 'Sparta' and 'Peloponnesian War'. This discovery confirmed her belief that this was Cole's room.

She was about to leave when she saw something tucked into the side of the rather gothic-looking vanity mirror. It was a picture of Cole Hollins, smiling and happy, with his arm around Maia.

Chapter Five

The picture of Maia and Cole was one of those touristy shots with the gaudily decorated, cardboard frames. A giant parrot was standing on Maia's gloved arm. She beamed at the camera, and Cole was grinning besottedly at her

Skylar was reaching for the photograph when she heard Chris call, "Skylar? Skylar? Do you give up?"

"No. Here I come." After one last look at the picture, she reluctantly left the room. Her sister's disappearance and the stories surrounding it made even less sense to her in light of the photo. The police ended their search for Maia after Martin Escalle presented them with a note, which was undeniably in Maia's handwriting. In the note, she indicated she was quitting without notice to elope with a man she'd met in the Keys. Skylar remembered Maia e-mailed her about a 'special guy' just before her disappearance, but there'd been no further word from her after that communication.

If Cole and Maia had been involved, it made it even more unlikely she had run off with some other guy. There was no way Skylar could imagine her sister involved with two men at the same time. The elopement letter was a ruse, and it had succeeded in getting the police away from Casa del Mar.

So, the question remained, where was Maia, now?

She was so caught up in her thoughts she almost missed the slight thump in the black lacquer Japanese chest. After sneaking up to it, she swung the door wide.

"Gotcha."

* * * *

Skylar wanted to talk to Angelique about inviting Conny's great nephew over to play with Chris. However, the older woman left for Miami before Skylar had a chance to ask. So, Lillian addressed Escalle on the matter, and he approved. The next Saturday, Connie's nephew dropped off Tyler, a sandy-haired, freckled boy with a puckish face and mischievous expression. There was something Huck Finn-esque about him, and Skylar liked him immediately.

Chris was less dazzled.

Ignoring the lack of rapport between the two boys, Skylar got them out on the basketball half-court. They started with a game of 'Horse,' but that failed to get them fired up. So, she lowered the hoop way down, so they could dunk. This turned out to be an inspired idea. The two boys pretended they were NBA superstars in the Slam Dunk contest. In no time, they were the best of friends.

Skylar was sure the companionship would be good for Chris, who spent all of his time with adults. He was way too serious and fearful.

When the boys were thoroughly red-faced and sweating, Tyler said, "Hey, let's go swimming."

"Tyler, we aren't going to go in the ocean today." Skylar debated how to handle this situation without shaming Chris.

Tyler looked at Chris. "Oh, yeah. Aunt Conny told me you're afraid of the water. That's no big deal. When I was little, I used to be afraid of thunder, but I'm not anymore. We can just go in the pool."

Skylar wanted to hug the big-hearted, little fellow and his great aunt, as well.

"I don't like swimming." Chris spoke very deliberately.

"You can watch me then. I know how to do cannon balls. Wanna see?"

She watched in amazement as the two boys went off to change into their swimsuits.

True to his word, Chris didn't get in the water. He simply sat and watched Tyler's antics.

The boy appeared indefatigable. He was in and out of the water performing a variety of signature flops and jumps. Both Skylar and Chris were in hysterics. Eventually, Chris relaxed enough to sit on the edge of the pool in the shallow end and dangle his feet in the water.

Skylar could see the light at the end of the tunnel. Maybe peer pressure would prove a force powerful enough to get Chris swimming, not that she wanted to make him into a follower, but she knew from her own experience as an athlete the presence of a peer can push you to demand more of yourself.

They were very late for lunch. The boys were also completely worn out. A less than thrilled Cole remarked later Chris had been falling asleep through his lessons.

Skylar easily dismissed the rebuke. She was pleased. She was making some progress on one front, at least. She liked Chris, and genuinely hoped she could help him.

That afternoon, she tried to read a book. She went for a long walk, but the lack of developments on her search for Maia was getting to her. She felt extremely anxious and frustrated. If Maia was still alive…

No, she couldn't think way. She was sure her sister was in trouble, and she had to get to her as soon as possible.

When she got back to the house, it was dark and quiet. She knew Lillian was running some errands, and the *Calypso* was not at dock, which meant Luke was also away. She had no idea where anyone else was.

Now was the time to take action.

She started on the lower level, peering into a game room, at the center of which stood an impressive cherry pool table. The next room was a home theater dominated by a giant, flat screen, plasma television. Further down the corridor, she encountered a music room that contained a golden harp and a grand piano. She wondered skeptically if any members of the Escalle household could play either instrument. She doubted it. The following room was a garden room filled with flowers and white wicker furniture set about a central water feature.

She heard a door shut somewhere in the house. As she headed back to her bedroom, she struggled with feelings of disappointment and futility. The rooms she entered were impersonal, bereft of any mementos, and of absolutely no use to her. In them, she could learn nothing of Escalle, his family, or his business. None yielded any clues about Maia's disappearance.

Then again if, as Maia hinted, Escalle was a criminal of some sort, why did Skylar, think she had the skills necessary to expose him? After all, the police failed to turn up anything when Maia went missing, and she was a complete amateur, just a gym teacher who was heartsick over having lost her only sister.

That evening, she dined with Connie and Lillian. Afterwards, restless and discouraged, she went for an evening stroll along the beach. She wondered where Escalle and his sister were. For that matter, where was Luke White and what was he up to?

She passed by the dock. The *Calypso* was still gone. Looking out over the water, she saw what she presumed was Escalle's yacht anchored at some distance from the shore. The vessel was still and dark against the setting sun.

It was peculiar. Why did Luke take her just so far out and then sit there? It had been the same the night before. It was unlikely he was up to some nefarious activity so close to the shoreline. It was more probable he was fishing.

She stared at the vessel. Suddenly, she had an idea and decided to act on it before she could change her mind.

After hurrying back to her room and changing into her bikini, she returned to the dock. She judged the distance to the boat couldn't be more than a couple of hundred yards. She stretched her arms forward. Her shoulders were tight from her morning swim, but she knew her muscles would loosen as they worked. She had easily swum greater distances in her prime. Granted, she did so swimming in a pool, but tonight, the ocean was still and calm. She could do it, she decided. She had to do it. For Maia.

Invigorated with her sense of purpose, she hit the water. Initially, she struggled to establish a rhythm, but soon her body responded to the challenge in the way it always had. She was cruising. A few times, she paused and raised her head out of the water to make sure she was on course.

When she was about twenty yards from the yacht, she stopped and treaded water. It was dark now, but the upper deck of the yacht was lit. She swam closer and treaded water again, this time for at least five minutes. Still, there was no movement. However, she could hear music playing. Who was onboard? Where was Luke? Was he somewhere inside? Was he alone?

What on earth was she going to do now?

She moved closer still, hoping to hear something. She was almost beside the motor yacht, when a masculine voice shouted down to her, but she couldn't understand what he said.

"Oh God," she muttered as the real danger of her situation struck her. She was at the mercy of whoever was on board the *Calypso*. She felt vulnerable and more than a little frightened. She hadn't understood what was said because of the water lapping against the side of the boat, but she had to answer. After all, she had been seen.

"What? What did you say?"

"Why don't you come up the swimming ladder?"

Now she recognized the deep, drawling tones. Luke was, indeed, on board the *Calypso*.

"Swim around to the transom platform."

With a pounding heart, she obeyed, though she had no idea how she was going to explain her presence. In the few seconds that passed before she was standing facing Luke, she didn't come up with an answer.

"Welcome, mermaid," he greeted her. "It's a little late for a swim, don't you think?"

She shivered in the chilly evening breeze. She could now hear the music clearly, and recognized Jimmy Buffet's scratchy but lyrical voice. At the moment, Jimmy was crooning about nothing remaining quite the same.

She took a deep breath, and inhaled the fragrant, heady aroma of a Cuban cigar. Luke flipped on the bridge lights, and they backlit him so he was a large shadow, except for the glowing red end of his smoke. His darkened form had the languorous grace of a predatory cat poised to pounce.

"You look cold," he drawled. "Or are you excited to see me?"

The cad was staring obviously at her erect nipples. Immediately, she crossed her arms over her chest. "Don't take it as a compliment. I'm puckered just about everywhere… Look, are you just going to stand there staring at me, or are you going to give me a towel?"

"Give me a minute, honey."

He disappeared into the yacht and returned moments later with a lush, terrycloth robe. She gratefully wrapped it around her wet body. As she tied the belt, she surreptitiously peeked at Luke. He had a two-day's growth of beard on his face and a tiny, golden hoop in one ear, and he was wearing a yellow surf shirt that said something about waxing his Johnson. A pair of faded, baggy shorts completed his ensemble.

To her dismay, she had to admit he looked delicious and naughty.

"You can't blame me for enjoying the view. Skylar Connelly, you are full of surprises."

She was very aware of his gaze moving up from her chest to her face. "How so?"

"Most of the gym teachers I know are dykes."

"Great, you're homophobic, too. What a Neanderthal."

"You'd be disappointed if I didn't say something like that. Seriously now, are you a lesbian?" He stepped closer to her.

"Geesh. Just let it go."

"Do you want to change into some dry clothes? I keep some stuff on board. I sleep out here a lot."

"Your clothes?"

"Unless you'd prefer Angelique's? Course she might not be too pleased about your borrowing her threads."

"Yours would be great." She'd feel less vulnerable dressed, and he wouldn't be able to stare at her nipples. She followed him mutely through a grand salon, into a small corridor, and then into a stateroom, but she couldn't really pay attention to her surroundings. She was too focused on the man in front of her. He had to have been some kind of athlete before he became a head of security/treasure hunter/criminal. He had the cutest buns.

"These okay?" After rifling through a dresser, he handed her a maroon V-neck T-shirt and a pair of sweats.

"Thanks." The clothes felt deliciously warm in her hands.

"You can change in here. I'll meet you up on deck."

About ten minutes later, she rejoined him up above. She had the hood on as it would take a while for the heavy mass of her hair to dry out. Luke was lying back in a deck chair, staring up at the night sky. Occasionally, he took sips of his Corona. "There's one for you on the table."

"Thanks." After picking up the beer, and noticing powerful binoculars on the table beside it, Skylar took the chaise lounge beside him. Refusing to show him that he intimidated her, she, too, stared upward and found the stars were brilliant and clear. As she gazed at the night sky, she caught a hint of spicy cologne on the evening breeze. She couldn't imagine a more romantic setting, or a sexier man, even though he sometimes played a jerk. She suspected there were hidden depths to Luke, but were those depths treacherous? Something in her protested that they weren't.

"You want to tell me what you're doing out here?"

"I felt like going for a swim. Having a goal makes going a distance more interesting. So, I chose the boat. I didn't know you were onboard."

"Yacht, please. Calling this beauty a 'boat' doesn't do her justice…For the record, I don't believe you didn't know I was out here. I think you knew and either came out here to spy on me, or to find me. So, I decided to accommodate your curiosity. That's why I called you aboard. Still, it's dangerous swimming at night by yourself. You got me thinking. In fact, I was wondering what you were up to from the moment you came out on the beach looking like a teenager's wet dream. That skimpy suit really got the old wheels spinning. I don't forget a hot bod, and I knew I had seen yours somewhere before. Then, I remembered."

Even though she had some idea what was coming, she still felt her stomach clench. She stared at him in the darkness. He hadn't moved an inch. He wasn't even looking at her, but she felt as if she was being gently stroked by his velvet voice.

"Do you mind telling me what an Olympic gold medallist is doing down here teaching some kid to swim?"

He sat up, leaning forward at the waist with his arms resting on his legs, and stared right at her.

It was a lazy posture, but she was aware of the energy and tension radiating from his large body.

Alarms started going off in her head warning: *Danger! Danger!*

She was totally at this guy's mercy. This far out on the water, she doubted anyone would hear her if she screamed. She glanced over the rail. If she made it to the water, she would be safe, but she was willing to bet he could move quickly if he was so inclined.

"Shit."

"That about sums it up."

"I'm not hiding anything," she argued defensively.

"Bullshit."

"It's all ancient history. Ten years ago, I swam in the Olympics. I got the gold medal mailed to me only after the two Chinese women who'd placed ahead of me were disqualified for steroid use."

"I read in *Sports Illustrated* you quit swimming because of what happened."

"I quit because I was over-the-hill. I got boobs and hips, and my times became slower and slower. So, I hung up my goggles and went to college. Now, I teach physical education and coach swimming."

"Why didn't you tell Escalle who you are?"

"You aren't hearing me, White. That was all a lifetime ago. No one really cares about it anymore. I don't want people to see me as some has-been. I want to be accepted for who I am now. My other qualifications were sufficient to get me this job."

"Oh come on. If I was a gold medallist, you can bet that would be right on the top of my resume."

"Look, swimming was my life, and my career ended badly for me. Swimmers are only popular the year before an Olympics. The rest of the time, the general public could care less about the sport.

"When I came in third, the media crucified me, and my sponsors dropped me like a hot potato. Then those Chinese girls were disqualified, and it didn't even matter anymore. All of the endorsement deals were gone. Yeah, I'm bitter about the whole thing. I didn't want to swim for the longest time. That was probably the worst part about it. I no longer enjoyed my very favorite thing to do, but you have to get on with your life.

"In time, I got back into the water, and it felt good again because there were no stopwatches or cameras. The pressure was gone." Skylar thought her explanation was convincing, mainly because it was the truth.

She wondered what would happen. Would he tell Escalle she swam out to the *Calypso* and get her fired? Would people start watching her? How would either development affect her search for Maia?

"Escalle would eat it up if he knew who you are."

"He knows who I am." She corrected tartly. "How did you recognize me?

He leaned closer, smirking at her. His golden brown eyes blazed with heat. "Babe, I never forget a pair of *bodacious tatas* and a nice, tight ass to go along with them."

"You are a complete pig."

He grinned. His white teeth glinted piratically in the moonlight. "Don't get your g-string in a wad, Skylar. I'll be serious. I knew I had seen you somewhere before, but until tonight, I couldn't place you. When I saw you out on the beach, it came to me. I had a roommate in college who was a swimmer. He had a poster of the women of the US swim team up over his bed. It was a *Sports Illustrated* layout, and you were in it. None of you were wearing tops. You had your arms crossed over your titties to show off your pipes. I can still picture you. You were kind of half-turned to the camera, with that long, dark hair of yours covering your chest. You were looking over your shoulder."

She knew the picture well. Her mother loathed it. She said it objectified the women of the US swim team, reduced them to sex objects.

"I had a top on, and so did some of the other girls. It was just strategically tucked."

"I couldn't see it, and I spent a lot of time staring at that picture when things were slow, or when I was recovering from a hangover… You were, and still are a hottie." He eyed her critically. "You've slimmed down some since then. You're a little softer looking. Your shoulders aren't quite so broad. Actually, you look better now.

"When you were walking toward the water, and you raised your arms to pull your hair back, the muscles on your arms and shoulders flexed. You looked so damned sexy, you took my breath away. It was like I was twenty again, and choking the chicken in my dorm room."

"I thought for a moment you were about to say something nice, and then you had to ruin it."

"Sugar, I would take it as a high compliment. Don't tell Brian, but you were my dream girl."

"Who's Brian?"

"My roommate. He had the hots for one of the other swimmers, a chunky, little, fireplug blonde. I spent a whole semester looking for a girl with a heart-shaped butt like yours. The kind that makes a man just wanta reach out and grab it." He demonstrated with his hands.

Despite herself, Skylar chuckled. "You're razzing me. I understand now. You enjoy giving me a hard time."

"No, honey," he stood up, then he straddled her chaise lounge so he was sitting directly in front of her. She drew her legs back on either side of the chair. He smelled of zesty cologne, salty sea air, beer, and man. It was a heady combination. Her insides began to melt like sun-warmed butter.

"I'd like to give you a long, hard, wet, unforgettable time." He reached out and stroked her cheek with his finger. "I wasn't kidding about you being my dream girl." He leaned slowly closer.

She knew what was coming but didn't stop him. Warm, masculine lips tentatively brushed her own. She reached up and cupped the nape of his neck, drawing him against her. Their breaths mingled, lips opened. The kiss deepened, grew hotter, hungrier, more demanding.

He placed both hands beneath either cheek of her butt and lifted her up onto his lap, bringing her astride him.

She groaned. Big, strong men who made her feel petite had always been her weakness. His hands kneaded her, and she was very aware of the hardness of his penis pressing into her sweatpants. When he pulled his mouth away from hers, she followed his lips longingly.

Chapter Six

"Easy sweetheart," Luke murmured. He trailed kisses along the line of her jaw, then licked and nuzzled his way up to a deliciously sensitive spot behind her ear.

She shivered with excitement and pleasure, and slid her hands along his muscled thighs and up his chest. He was all hard, firm planes beneath her questing fingers. She wriggled still closer to him, and kissed and nibbled her way up his neck and back to his lips.

When their lips met once more, their tongues parried back and forth erotically, but he didn't rush. Clearly, a man who enjoyed the act of kissing, he took his time, allowing the passion between them to grow.

Suddenly, a phone rang. At first, he ignored it, but it rang again and again insistently.

"You should probably answer that," she muttered. Sitting back, she tried to regain control and put some distance between them. What was she doing? She barely knew this man and certainly didn't trust him. There were so many reasons why she shouldn't make love with him, but she had forgotten all of them when he held her in his arms.

"Ummm." He reached out to draw her back to him.

"What if it's Escalle?"

Saying their employer's name out loud effectively ended the moment.

"I expect it is," Luke muttered in frustration. "I should have turned off my cell phone." He awkwardly stood up. Shifted his shorts around a little, and then headed up the steps to the pilothouse.

Once he was gone, Skylar shivered. What was she doing? It had admittedly been a while since she had had a lover, but her reaction was ridiculous. Granted, the man was fatally sexy with an irreverent intelligence. He was also an exceptional kisser with a devilishly delightful way of touching her. But there was no point in thinking about him in this way. The man was a treasure hunter, and possibly a criminal. She knew nothing about him, nothing about his background.

All she knew was that with one kiss, one touch, he made her wet and wanting. That probably only proved he was an accomplished ladies' man, but then she recalled his heart had been pounding as frantically as her own under her fingertips. His kisses had been just as needy.

For all she knew, he might have done something with or to Maia.

He headed back down the steps. "We won't be bothered again, but we don't have much time."

"No, Luke. I don't think this is a good idea. Could you take me back to shore? It's rather dark to swim back, and I'm tired."

"Sweetheart." He reached out to touch her, and she stepped back.

"No. I mean, this is just not happening. I'm not looking for anything right now."

To her surprise, he chuckled. "You may not have been looking, but we sure found something."

"Let's forget about this."

"Honey, I plan on making you forget a whole bunch of things, for a little while, but not this, definitely not this. If you want to stew and worry, that's your prerogative. It won't change anything."

"I can't talk to you. You just don't listen."

"You're wrong there. I hear you loud and clear. I'm like the guy Mel Gibson plays in that movie. I know what women want. I know you want me, but something is bothering you, holding you back. You ought to get it off your chest. I figure you will when the time is right.

"Until then, I can wait. You're worth it. But as I was trying to tell you, I have to get back to the house. So, I'll take a rain check on this argument, even though it turns me on to see you all hot and bothered.

"Now, you can either join me in the pilot house, or you can stay out here. I'll understand if you're a little nervous about being in a small room with me, but I have to concentrate, so you'll have to keep your hands off of me."

She smiled. He really was too outrageous. "I'll go up with you. It's getting a little cool down here... Half of the time, I can't tell if you're serious or just kidding around. I hope you're kidding. Otherwise, you really do have an over inflated sense of self-worth."

"No, Skylar." He caressingly drawled out her name. "When it comes to you, girl, I'm not just foolin'. We have some pretty powerful chemistry between us."

The whole way back to Casa del Mar, Luke was charming and impossible to pin down on any subject. He deftly sidestepped all of her inquiries about his past and his present. He distracted her by pointing out some constellations, which had once been important to sailors, and he teased and told stories until they docked.

"Skylar," he suddenly said as she prepared to disembark.

She hesitated, and he reached out and took her hand. He tugged her down off the steps and back against him. He tilted her chin up, and dusted her lips with a feather light promise of a kiss.

She resisted the urge to pull him back for more.

"Honey, we'll talk about all of this real soon."

Though every cell in her body screamed in protest, she pulled away from him. "There's nothing to discuss. I'm only here for a couple of months, and I'm not looking for a fling."

"You think too much. Just let the magic happen."

"You sound like a margarita ad."

His white teeth flashed in a grin. "Bye, sweetheart."

Skylar realized she'd been dismissed, and she'd allowed him to distract her from her goal. "Where do you have to go right now? It's late for a business meeting."

"I'm going to pick up a few associates for Mr. Escalle."

"When did he get back?"

He took a step closer to her. "I want you to really hear me, Skylar. Asking questions around here is a dangerous business. Take my advice, teach the boy to swim, sightsee, and don't mess with anything else, including the *Calypso*. You're just lucky I was the one out on her tonight. What would you have done if it had been Stevens? He's one tough SOB, and he doesn't have much respect for women. I don't know what you're looking for, but stop it now, before it's too late."

The devil-may-care-southern boy was gone. A dead-serious stranger stared at her.

"Too late for what?"

"Let it go, Skylar. You don't want to know. See ya."

With that, he turned his back on her and walked away.

She watched him head back up to the pilothouse. She fought a nearly irresistible desire to go after him, to try and push him to tell her more, to explain his warning. She knew doing so would be even more suspicious. He already suspected she had ulterior motives in coming to Casa del Mar. He might very well go to his employer about her. Her search for Maia would be well and truly over.

Then there was the issue of the red-hot attraction between them. Should she trust her instincts about Luke? If he really had something to do with her sister's disappearance, she couldn't be so attracted to him. She mulled over all these issues as she headed back to the house.

* * * *

Skylar's days settled into a comfortable routine. She genuinely liked Chris. He was a pretty decent basketball and tennis player, and she discovered he had real talent for golf on an outing to the nearby country club course.

He appeared to be greatly benefiting from the time with Tyler. She was pleased to see Chris drop his adult-like manner and laugh and goof off like any other kid when Tyler was around.

With respect to swimming, Chris was gradually coming to trust her. He was now kicking around the shallow end of the pool with a floaty. She planned to introduce the techniques of certain strokes in the near future. All in all, working with him was enjoyable and rewarding, if not particularly challenging.

Her investigation into her sister's disappearance was barely making any headway. She was sure something peculiar was going on at Casa del Mar. People arrived at all hours to see Escalle, but, invariably, these meetings took place in Escalle's office, and she would just glimpse the strangers coming and going.

One afternoon, she was heading down the second floor corridor on her way to the kitchen to get a soda when she heard voices in the entrance foyer. Escalle was speaking loudly and jocularly in Spanish with some other men. He was obviously not concerned about being overheard.

For a moment, she wished she'd taken Spanish rather than French in school, but then she had an idea. She sprinted back to her room, hoping her running footsteps weren't audible from downstairs. She snatched her camera from where it lay atop the dresser and hurried back down the hall in the opposite direction from which she came. The door to Angelique's meditation room was ajar. She burst through. "Please be opened. Please be opened," she chanted as she reached for the knob on the French doors, which led out onto the balcony. "Yes."

She stepped out. This little porch offered a breathtaking view of the sea if one looked straight out. However, if one looked down and a little to the left, one had a clear view of the driveway leading into the parking area. Nearly holding her breath with anticipation, hoping she wasn't too late, she waited.

She wasn't disappointed. Bill Stevens appeared first. He was closely followed by two other men, one of whom was a bodyguard-type, so muscle-bound he couldn't put his arms down flat at his sides. She snapped a few pictures before they disappeared from view. She waited. A black Mercedes exited the parking area, she was too high up and the windows of the car were too darkly tinted to get any more shots.

Well pleased, she closed the door leading out to the balcony. It finally felt like she was doing something proactive to look into Maia's disappearance. As she headed back out into the corridor, she fiddled with her lens cap, trying to fit it to her camera. She had long ago lost the original lens cap that came with the camera. She'd purchased a new one, but it had never quite fit right. She was so engrossed that she walked right into Cole Hollins.

"Oh, geez. I'm sorry. I wasn't looking where I was going."

"No harm done." He smiled at her. "I wasn't paying attention either. I was reading." He held up the leather bound, gold embossed book. "I've had this terrible habit of reading while walking since I was child." He glanced rather pointedly at her camera. "Are you a photographer?"

"No, not really. I mean, I'm not an expert by any means. I just like taking pictures. The view from the balcony in there is incredible. The sea and the sky just take your breath away. I was trying to get a decent panoramic shot. If I do, I might blow it up to poster size and put it on my wall at home."

"I'd like to see your pictures. Photography is a hobby of mine. I subscribe to *Shutterbug* magazine. I don't mean to be arrogant, but I might be able to share some insights I've garnered from my own efforts and from articles I've read."

"That would be great," she lied with an overly bright smile. "I wish I'd gotten a sail boat against the sky line. Well, I'll just have to try again some other time," she ad-libbed, hoping this story would provide her with a reasonable explanation should Cole encounter her in the meditation room armed with her camera again.

"I know some spots with sensational views. I could share them with you."

"I'd enjoy that," she responded enthusiastically. "But, right now, I really do have to focus on working on my thesis in my free time. I hope to be finished in a few weeks, and then I'll be free more. Maybe we could do something then?"

"That would be delightful. Well, if you will excuse me…"

"What are you reading?"

"*The Satyrcon.*"

"Excuse me?"

"By Petronius. He was a Roman. It's a satire."

He was observing her with the sort of amazed and appalled look the very erudite cast upon the unlettered. Feeling rather ignorant and uncouth, she muttered: "Oh. Sounds interesting."

"It is… Well, I'll see you at dinner."

"Bye."

As Skylar walked back to her room, she passed several rooms she was very eager to get into, among them were Escalle's bedroom and his library. She couldn't come up with any plausible reason for entering her employer's boudoir. The library was a more public room, and she had received permission to borrow books from the shelves. Invariably, whenever she entered it, there was someone else around, a maid dusting or Lillian bringing in a flower arrangement. It seemed the coast was never clear.

She finally had the opportunity to really snoop a few days later, on a Sunday afternoon. She was off for the day, and Escalle and his family had gone out on the *Calypso* for a deep-sea fishing trip. She had felt terrible for Chris. He had been sobbing and pleading with his mother to let him stay behind. Yvette went along, as did Lillian. Conny went also.

Luke was captaining the vessel, assisted by a small crew. Even Skylar had been invited, but she passed on the cruise, saying she was too busy with her thesis. She knew Bill Stevens was away as well. He left earlier that morning on some business matter for Escalle.

In other words, this afternoon offered her the perfect opportunity for some serious snooping.

She waited until the *Calypso* was a dark shape along the horizon, then she hurried down the hall to the master suite. She knocked lightly, and tested the door handle. She opened the door and peered in.

The space was huge and elegantly masculine. It was decorated in rich burgundies, deep linens, and golds. One entire side of the room consisted of windows, and offered a breathtaking view of the ocean. It was broken into two sections, a seating area with a wet bar and mahogany encased entertainment center and a sleeping area dominated by a magnificent four-poster bed. A built in bookshelf bridged the two sections. It was filled with books with titles like *The Charge of the Light Brigade, The Battle of the Bulge,* and *Gettysburg, the Untold Story.* But She could see nothing useful in her search for Maia.

Desperate to find some clue, she passed through the dressing room and the bathroom. There was a door at the far end of the bathroom, which led into a more feminine, smaller one. Unlike the suite she had just passed through, here white towels were tossed haphazardly about.

The adjoining dressing room was in an even worse state of disarray. An endless assortment of cosmetics, empty glasses, opened jewelry cases, and hair care products were scattered about. The room positively reeked of Poison, Yvette's signature scent.

The bedroom was equally trashed. The bed was unmade. The floor was littered with clothing and shoes. Skylar did not even know where to start looking for information about her sister.

She was frankly surprised Lillian allowed these rooms to be in this condition. She was a superb housekeeper, on top of everything that went on at Casa del Mar, and thoroughly devoted to Martin Escalle.

Perhaps the condition of the suite indicated Yvette's stock was falling with Escalle?

Feeling pressed for time, Skylar exited Yvette's and Escalle's respective suites, making sure to close all the doors behind her. The house remained Sunday-afternoon still as she stole down the main staircase. Again, she cautiously knocked on the library doors before opening them and heading in.

The dark green curtains hadn't been drawn back from the windows, and the magnificent cherry paneled room was dim. A skylight bathed the desk area in golden light, highlighting an elegantly streamlined, silver laptop. It beckoned to her, and she obediently hurried over and sat down.

To her amazement, the computer was on, and the mouse responded to her touch. The screen asked for her 'username'. She typed in 'Martin Escalle'. The name was not recognized. She tried 'Escalle' and 'Martin,' with no success. After about five minutes, swearing under her breath in frustration, she pivoted the chair away from the laptop.

Now, she pulled open desk drawers, none of which were locked. Everything was neat and orderly and useless to her. There were some hanging files in one drawer, but they just contained some information about what appeared to be perfectly legal investments in well-known companies. There was a file that included newspaper articles about Escalle. One detailed his charitable efforts made through one of his companies, Escalle Imports. There was another article which described a condominium building project in which he was a major player. There was nothing incriminating, nothing that looked remotely illegal.

Damn and double damn. She was well aware, if the man was up to no good, it was highly unlikely he would just leave evidence lying about, but she had hoped for something.

A search of the file cabinets behind the desk proved equally fruitless. Resting her chin on the heel of her hand, she was staring morosely about, wondering if there was a safe hidden somewhere in the room, when she noticed the corner of a piece of paper sticking up out of the paper shredder atop the waste paper can and reached for it.

"What the hell are you doing in here?" Bill Stevens growled from the doorway.

Skylar jumped in surprise, and, turning to face him, she pretended to reach back to adjust the elastic waistband of her short, billowy skirt, tucking the paper in as she did so.

"Hi, Bill. I was looking for a book to read. Mr. Escalle said I could borrow books from in here." She knew she was babbling.

Of course, his gaze immediately became fixed on the computer. "Have you been messing with the boss' laptop?"

"It was on. I was just looking at it. It's really an awesome machine but I didn't go into any files or anything."

He walked over to the desk, and turned the computer so it faced him. He moved the mouse around, and straightened when it appeared he was satisfied she hadn't successfully accessed information saved on the machine.

"Bill, I was in here to get a book. The laptop was just sitting out, and it is the top of the line model."

He pushed one desk drawer more deeply into its slot. Her heart sunk. He was onto her. He knew she had been snooping around.

"You done in here?"

Surprisingly, it appeared he wasn't going to confront her.

"Oh yes. I think I am."

"What about your book?" he remarked sarcastically.

She thought quickly. "I've always wanted to read *Poland* by Michener." She headed directly to the shelf where she returned the book only days before, but Stevens didn't know that. "Yes, this is where I saw it... I'll see you later, Bill."

He followed her out into the hallway. She felt him watching her as she proceeded down the hall.

She made herself walk slowly and pretend to read the inside flap of the book until a bend in the corridor hid her from view. Then, she dropped all pretense and ran the rest of the way to her room. After she locked the door, she flopped down on her bed and pulled the piece of paper out from her waistband.

The note was handwritten on lined, yellow legal paper. It consisted of three names: Ramon Pinell, Anthony Urbino, and an Oscar. Oscar's surname wasn't on the scrap.

Skylar was disappointed. She'd hoped to find something really conclusive about Escalle and his operations. The fact Stevens discovered her snooping made this piece of paper potentially very expensive in terms of consequences for her. Still, though she had no idea who these persons were, it seemed possible they were associates of Escalle's in his illegal business activities.

One thing was certain, she couldn't keep either the bit of paper or the pictures she'd taken the other day in her room. If they were valuable in some way, maybe by helping to establish a connection between Escalle and some known criminals, they could prove very dangerous to her.

She decided to drive into Key West as soon as possible and get a safety deposit box. She would keep one key and send the other to her best friend, Laura, along with a letter detailing the location of the box and directions to forward the contents to law enforcement in the event something happened to her.

That possibility was becoming more likely. Now, Luke and Bill Stevens had reason to be suspicious of her. She had no way of knowing who were the bad guys and who were the good guys. But, she'd come to the Florida Keys to find out what had happened to Maia, and she wouldn't let her concerns about her own well-being weaken her resolve. For her sister's sake, she would persevere.

She also decided she would continue to add to the safety deposit box by taking pictures of future guests to Casa del Mar. Her mother had taught her 'if you sleep with pigs, you get dirty.' If Escalle was up to no good, then it seemed very likely to Skylar there might be documented bad guys in the endless parade of visitors to Casa del Mar. Perhaps the police could figure out what was going on at the beachside estate if she presented them with a cast of characters.

* * * *

A few days later, Skylar got an e-mail from Laura confirming the package arrived. She'd debated how much to tell Laura. Her best friend was no shrinking violet. Though she could be absolutely counted on, Skylar knew she would call in reinforcements by contacting Skylar's mother if she became seriously worried. If her mother got involved…

The phone rang and she glanced over at the cream telephone on the bedside table. Who could be calling? She hadn't given her phone number to anyone.

Her parents knew she was in the Keys, but they thought she was off on a rustic teachers' retreat. She made a point of calling them on her cell phone once a week, so they wouldn't worry.

"Skylar, Lillian here. This evening, Mr. Escalle and Angelique are having some guests over for cocktails and dinner. It will all be *al fresco,* and as the weather looks lovely, it should be very pleasant. You are welcome to join us. The attire is casual dressy."

"That sounds great, Lillian. I'll look forward to it."

"Good. I'll see you this evening. *Ciao.*"

Skylar pondered this strange turn of events as she set down the phone. Stevens must not have discussed the library incident with his boss. But why not? She didn't trust him for a minute, and suspected he'd bring the whole thing up when it best suited him.

Still, a dinner party was unlikely to provide him with the right moment, and it would present her with the opportunity to meet some of Escalle's connections. She intended to add these names to her stash in the safety deposit box.

Feeling energized, she jumped up off the bed and headed into the shower. She wondered if Luke would be at the party. She certainly hoped so, for she intended to dress to kill. She'd always found a man was generally more talkative with a woman he wanted to seduce, and she needed to get Luke to explain his involvement in Escalle's organization.

She chose to wear a long, clingy, red chiffon dress and strappy sandals, which had three-and-a-half inch heels. She styled her hair so it lay thick and curly over her shoulders and down her back, and she went for an exotic look with her cosmetics. Then, she studied her reflection in the full-length bathroom mirror. One toned arm and shoulder were bared by the draping of the gown. The ankle length skirt was cut on the bias, and when she moved, the long and, she hoped, sexy line of her thigh was revealed. She was going for fascinating and dangerous, the better to throw Luke off balance.

Something was missing. Her necklace. She had forgotten to put it back on after her shower. After securing it around her neck, she stroked the figure of the sleek golden dolphin leaping through a silver hoop. Maia had sent it to her as a birthday present just after arriving in Key West. Since her sister's disappearance, Skylar always wore it.

By the time she sauntered out to the veranda, the party was in full swing. To her surprise, this was no small gathering. She guessed there were between thirty and forty people in attendance, and she recognized only a few. There was even a group of musicians playing upbeat Spanish music.

She caught sight of Luke almost immediately. He stood a few inches taller than most of the other men, and his golden mane was unmistakable. He was dancing with Yvette, who was literally draped all over him.

Skylar tried to deliberately quash a quick, ugly surge of jealousy. If he wanted Yvette, that was his business. Still, it wasn't a very clever thing to be doing in front of his employer.

"They dance well together." Cole echoed her unhappy thoughts as he appeared at her elbow. He held a margarita glass in each hand and offered one to her. "I saw you come in. Enjoy."

"Thank you. It was kind of you to think of me."

"I can't take credit for a big effort. Do you see that waitress there? She's carrying around a whole tray of these. I simply lightened her load."

Cole looked handsome in an Ivy League, Martha's Vineyard sort of way. His thinning hair was still damp and brushed straight back from his pronounced brow. His white oxford shirt set off his dark tan, but he did nothing for her. It was the sexy pirate on the dance floor who made her pulse race...

"I am really impressed with the work you are doing with Chris. He really likes playing... Oh, excuse me, I mean learning with you."

Skylar smiled at him. "It is playing, and I'm not embarrassed to admit it. Kids learn best through play."

"You're doing a fine job." He met her glance and then stared at her. "Your eyes...they're green."

"They are."

"I... I...They remind me of someone else's."

"Whose?"

He seemed flustered. "There was a young woman who worked here before you. She left rather suddenly. At the time, we..." It appeared he couldn't complete his thoughts. All his usual ease with words and cultured fluidity of speech disappeared.

Skylar struggled to contain her excitement. She was very close to getting real information on Maia.

"You two had a relationship?"

"It would be an exaggeration to describe it as a relationship, but there was something between us. At least, I thought we had something…until she simply vanished."

"Vanished? Are you serious? What happened?" Skylar trembled as she waited for the answer. "What was her name?"

Chapter Seven

"Her name?" Cole said, "Her name? It was Ma—"

"Cole, Skylar, please join us." Angelique broke in with no apparent discomfort that she was interrupting a conversation.

Skylar glared at Angelique in irritation. The woman had the worst timing. She was sure Cole had been close to confiding in her.

"This is a dear friend of mine, Lydia Davis. Lydia has just been asking about Chris. I've been telling her all about the fabulous progress he's been making with the two of you. Lydia has two children of her own."

"My Mackenzie and Austin attend St. John's Academy in Miami," Lydia announced. She was a silicone enhanced, leather skinned woman of about forty-five. Her smiling face was nearly expressionless due to a few too many facial surgeries and liberal use of Botox.

"Chris will be going off to Pine View School in Palm Beach this fall. We, Martin and I, thought it best to school him at home after Jim's death. It was quite traumatic for a boy of his age, for all of us."

"You poor dear. You're so brave, raising your son as a single parent."

"I haven't been totally on my own. Martin has been a fine role model for Chris. We've been so fortunate in finding help to work with Chris." Angelique cued Cole and Skylar with a glance.

"Christopher is a very bright and talented young man. He's coming along quite well in his academic program of study. He is very advanced, particularly in mathematics, for a child of his age." Cole responded appropriately. All traces of his earlier discomfiture were gone. Now, he was displaying only polished manners and polite interest.

"Angie, it must free you up so much to have a staff of three just for your son. My children run circles around our nanny.”

A strange expression flitted across Angelique’s face. The other woman’s words didn’t please her. “Cole and Skylar tutor Chris for a few hours each day, and Conny, his nanny, is a dear, and we could never let her go. I treasure my time with Chris. I’ll really miss him when he’s at school. He’s getting to be such a big boy, but he still likes me to read to him at night. I think that is my favorite time of the day, when I get my baby all to myself.”

This was news to Skylar, who had not expected Angelique to be a very interested mother. She would have guessed Conny performed bedtime duties for the boy.

“You’re such a little domestic at heart.”

“Jim and I wanted a big family.”

“Consider it a blessing you only have the one. My second absolutely ruined my figure.” Lydia smiled, and it appeared almost painful how her eyes attempted but couldn’t succeed in drawing up at the corners. She glanced over at Skylar. “Now I understand this completely delicious young man teaches Chris his academic subjects, but what do you do?”

“I’m working with him on his gross motor development.”

“What, dear?” The woman had no idea what she was talking about

“I teach him sports skills and swimming.”

“Oh, swimming.” Understanding dawned in Lydia’s eyes as she raised one hand with French manicured nails to her cheek. “With the tragedy and everything, I never would have guessed that poor child would ever go near the water.”

“Skylar is working with Chris to address his fear,” Angelique offered. “I was worried about it at first. I didn’t think pushing the swimming thing was a good idea, but Chris tells me he doesn’t mind the lessons, and that is about as enthusiastic an endorsement as I’m going to get. You know how boys are.”

“Since Tyler started participating in the swimming lessons, Chris has really come along. He was treading water in the deep end of the pool yesterday.” Cole said.

“Tyler?” Angelique questioned cluelessly.

“Conny’s great nephew,” Skylar explained. “He’s a nice kid, and having him along has really pushed Chris to overcome his fears.”

"You've been shaming my son in front of another child to get him to swim. How dare you!"

"It's not like that at all. Sometimes other children are the best motivators."

"Why didn't you discuss this with me?"

Skylar had to bite her tongue to keep from asking how or when.

"If you'll excuse me," Lydia demurred. "Paul is trying to get my attention."

"How long has this been going on behind my back?" Angelique demanded.

"Didn't Chris tell you?" Skylar let slip the catty remark.

"What? Who do you think you are?"

"Angelique, Skylar, what seems to be amiss?" Martin Escalle remarked as he tucked a protective arm through his sister's.

"Martin, do you know what this woman has been doing to Chris?"

"What, my dear?"

"She's been having a strange boy come here, to force Chris into the water, to make him swim."

"I think it's wonderful Chris is learning to interact with a peer. Having the other child around has proven a clever strategy. Just yesterday, I observed part of the lesson from the library window. Chris is making remarkable progress. I know you're not a morning person, Angelique, but you really should watch sometime."

"You knew about this? And you didn't tell me?"

"You've been so busy planning the charitable ball."

"Nothing is more important to me than my son. You know that, Martin." She appeared genuinely upset because she'd been left out of a decision regarding her son.

Skylar was tempted to revise her opinion of the woman. It now seemed clear she was an interested if preoccupied mother.

"Do you trust my judgment?" Martin questioned his sister. His expression was patient but chiding.

"Of course, I do, Martin, but…"

"We should be mingling, my dear. What must our guests be thinking? Cole, Skylar." With a nod to each, he led Angelique back into the thick of things.

"That didn't go well." Skylar remarked to Cole.

"Don't blame yourself. You were just doing your job. Martin should have kept her updated."

Martin, not Mr. Escalle, she noted. "All she had to do was walk out to the pool. We weren't exactly hiding anything."

"I know. Don't worry. He thinks you're doing a great job, and he's the one you have to please."

"But she's Chris' mother."

"Martin calls all the shots. I think Angelique would like to be more involved in decisions concerning Chris, but she's always so busy volunteering. You see, it's important for Martin's business that the family be visible in the community. That's Angelique's job. Think I'm going to get another drink. Come on over with me. Yours looks like it needs to be refreshed."

She allowed him to lead her through the crowd toward the bar. Cole insisted she give up on her now rather tired margarita and try a hurricane. As she leaned the small of her back up against the bar, she gazed out at the gathering. Waitresses and waiters carried past an endless bounty of seafood delicacies. Once the alcohol mellowed her mood, she chatted with several other guests. To her surprise, she found she was enjoying herself. There were only two downers: Luke had yet to speak with her, and Angelique was obviously still irate with her.

Too bad for both of them. She was having fun. She realized she'd probably had a few too many cocktails, but she wasn't drunk. Cole was a very pleasant companion. He had stayed by her side throughout the evening.

Unfortunately, his presence had not managed to deflect the attention of a stocky, short, dark haired fellow who kept eyeing her hungrily. Finally, just as the dinner buffet was being cleared, and coffee, desert, and sweet, chilled, after dinner wines were being brought out, he approached her.

"I am Saul Petr, lovely lady. What is your name?" He raised her hand to his lips and kissed it.

"Skylar Connelly."

"I am delighted and enchanted to make your acquaintance."

She fought the urge to giggle. Petr was a good six inches shorter than she was in her heels, and he made no effort to meet her glance. Instead, he was staring quite obviously at her breasts. She caught sight of Luke. He was now standing with Yvette not far from the bar against which she leaned. His expression could only be described as menacing.

Too bad, she decided as she lifted the heavy fall of hair from her neck, baring hot, damp skin to the evening breeze. He had no right to judge her behavior. It was not like they had an exclusive relationship, and he'd been glued to Ms. Silicone Breasts' side all evening. The music changed from a pulsing Mariachi beat to a lilting, melodic love song.

"Would you care to dance with me?" Saul questioned.

So you can bury your face in my breasts? she wanted to ask, but she saw Luke was still watching her, so she said, "Yes, that would be nice."

He led her out to the dance floor. She refused to slouch, to make the shorter man more comfortable. She wanted him to be aware they weren't well-matched. Skylar also held her arms out, so he would hold her at a distance. To her dismay, he sought to pull her full up against him. She leaned back against his hold, but found him both strong and determined. His heavy, musky cologne made her eyes water. Apparently oblivious to the music, he sought to grind his pelvis against her thigh. She was about to walk off the dance floor, when he abruptly drew away from her.

Skylar realized Luke was standing beside them.

"Petr, the lady promised me this dance." Luke looked impossibly appealing, handsome, large, confident, and virile.

"She said nothing about this to me."

"Oh, I forgot. I guess I've had too many margaritas tonight. Sorry for the confusion. Saul, I did promise this dance to Luke." She suddenly felt as if she were a character in an Austen novel. Unlike Austen's heroines, however, she didn't carry a little dance card for her suitors to sign, so she was very safe in her lie.

"You are dancing with me." Saul sought to draw her back into his embrace. She resisted, smiling broadly all the while in order to diffuse the situation. Their threesome was attracting attention, and anger suffused Petr's face.

"I mean no disrespect, Señor Petr, but the lady and I have an understanding. This is our song."

Skylar, for one, had no idea what the name of this rather elevator-esque instrumental piece was. She would have to ask the band before she left. For, apparently, it was now 'their song'.

Comprehension dawned in the small, dark eyes. "I did not know she was yours. If she were my woman, I would guard her more carefully."

"I intend to." With that, Luke stepped up to her and swept her into his arms.

Now she was Scarlet, being propelled across the floor in Rhett's arms at the Fundraising Ball. In contrast to Petr, Luke held her loosely, allowing her to choose the distance between them. She leaned close, wrapping her arms around his neck, allowing her body to align with his. She was well aware the alcohol probably diminished her inhibitions, and she was playing with fire. But, for tonight, she didn't care.

He pressed her closer still. Their bodies moved as one. Her head was nestled against his neck, between his jaw and his collarbone. Her now sensitive breasts pressed against the hard planes of his chest. His long, powerful thighs were entwined with her own. It was easy to follow his steps. The man had a careless confidence of rhythm, which communicated itself through his body to hers. He felt delicious, and so right.

Skylar giggled. She resisted the urge to reach down and grasp his butt in her hands.

"What's so funny?" he murmured into her hair.

"You have a fabulous butt."

He drew back enough so he could stare into her eyes. "My, my, we are outrageous tonight. What's with the change in attitude?"

"You rescued me from little Napoleon."

"I'll probably get grief about it later, but I think it was well worth it to have you owe me." He drew her back against him and allowed his hands to rest low on her waist. He began to lightly stroke the small of her back.

She reached down and grasped his hands, moving them to a more respectable, less titillating position. "It's not like you saved me from a burning building or anything. I don't owe you much."

"I don't know," he teased. "Petr is one nasty dude, not someone you want to cross. He tends to get fixated on what he wants."

"He went away as soon as you told him…"

"That you were my woman." He finished the thought for her, knowing she wouldn't be comfortable saying it. "I had to make it clear to him you're taken."

"I'm not afraid of him."

"You should be. He's a dangerous man."

"What do you mean?"

"He's ruthless. People who get in his way don't do well."

"What sort of business is he in?" she mumbled, trying to follow the thread of the conversation, for Maia's sake, but losing herself in the sensual pleasure of holding him.

"He's an associate of Escalle's."

"Meaning?"

"He's in the import and export business."

"I'll bet that means he's moving either guns or drugs." The words were out of her mouth before she could stop them.

He stiffened in her arms. "How did you...We have to talk."

His tone was deadly serious.

She tilted her head back. Green eyes clashed with brown ones. "I'm right, aren't I? Escalle is a..."

"Stop it." Though he spoke in a whisper, his words were a direct order. "Not here," he pleaded. He leaned back, gentling her against him. She closed her eyes and allowed the moment to consume her. Of their own volition, her lips moved against his neck in time with the seductive rhythm of the music.

The song was winding down, but she was loath to release him. It seemed as if he shared her feelings, for even after the last note had died away, he held onto her. When he finally withdrew from her, she felt cold, naked, and bereft.

"Come with me."

She nodded acquiescence.

He kept her hand, and led her off the veranda toward the beach.

"Just give me a minute." She reached down and took off her sandals. She carried them in her hands as they headed out onto the silver moonlit beach. The sand was cool and granularly smooth under her feet.

"Let's sit here. Wait. Here, sit on my coat." He removed his obviously expensive jacket and laid it down on the sand.

"That's very chivalrous of you," she commented as she sat down. The silk lining of the coat remained deliciously warm with his body heat.

He sat down very close beside her, and casually draped an arm over her shoulders. "My mother's a southern bell. She would give me hell if I let a pretty lady sit in the sand when I had a jacket handy."

"I don't want to ruin it or anything."

"Forget about it, Skylar. It's just sand. It'll shake out."

They sat still, taking in the view of the moon reflected on the shiny obsidian of the night sea. The party music had faded into a distant murmur, nearly drowned out by the water sounds. She shivered and drew closer to the warmth he radiated. He reached out and touched her chin very gently, turning her so they were looking into each other's eyes again. She closed hers before their lips met. The kiss started out gentle and tender. It became progressively hungrier, more demanding. Soon, he was pressing her back down onto his coat, using his large body to cover and to warm her.

The man was an unbelievable kisser. Skylar usually found kissing rather overrated. It was something you did before you progressed to the more interesting stuff. But this man's kiss was something to savor, something to drown in, to lose one's self in. His body was hard everywhere it came into contact with hers, and he smelled heavenly. He nuzzled her neck, then nibbled delicately on her earlobe. Then asked, "What do you know about Escalle?"

"Um… What?"

"Escalle. What do you know about his business?"

"What? Escalle? You jerk." Using both of her hands, she pushed him off her and abruptly sat up. "Don't try to pump me. I'm not a fool."

He reclined back in the sand. He wasn't chagrined in the least. "I don't take you for a fool. I was merely employing my powers of persuasion."

"I can't trust you." Dusting herself off, she started to get up.

He caught her hand. "It's not like you weren't trying the same thing on me, sweetheart."

"I…You…Just leave me alone."

"We have to talk. You don't know what you're getting into. I can't protect you unless I know what you're up to. What are you doing here, Skylar? The truth this time."

"Why should I tell you the truth when you won't tell me anything?"

"You show me yours, I'll show you mine."

"Could you please try to behave as if you had greater maturity than the average twelve-year-old?"

"I can try, but I can't promise you anything. My mother says my maturation was arrested in my early teen years."

"Why am I not surprised?"

"Seriously, what do you know about Escalle?"

"What do you know?" she countered yet again.

"Enough to tell you to stay out of his business. People who get in his way have a nasty habit of disappearing."

She immediately thought of Maia. "Who disappeared?"

"You don't believe me. You're a hardheaded woman. Honestly, I know of several people. Business associates, Angelique's husband, a girl who was here last summer. They all leave, or drown, or vanish very mysteriously. I don't want you to become one of them. I like you, Skylar. For your own sake, quit this job. Go home."

Chapter Eight

"Why? What are you telling me?"

"I can't tell you anything. Just trust me."

"Why should I trust you?"

"Because of this." He leaned into her. Their lips met, and Skylar found herself lost again. Her anger and her frustration transformed into passion. She reached for and yanked at his shirt buttons. She slid a hand down and over the hard ridge of his arousal. He groaned as he caressed his way up her thighs, raising her skirt as he went.

Maia. The thought of her sister recalled her to herself.

"Wait. This girl who disappeared, who was she?"

"A college kid. Story was she ran away with some guy. I know it's not true. Now, when are you going to quit?"

"What happened to the girl?"

"She..."

Just then, the tranquility of the night was shattered by a woman's scream.

"What?"

"Come on."

Luke was already up. Skylar shoved on her sandals. They ran back in the direction of the party. He released her hand as they arrived at the veranda.

The band continued to play, but no one was dancing. Guests milled about whispering, or stood in shocked silence staring. Yvette was audibly sobbing and completely hysterical. Bill Stevens was holding her back by both of her arms. Martin Escalle was standing in front her. He was using a monogrammed handkerchief to wipe a white concoction from his face.

"Ah, Luke." Escalle noticed the other man immediately. "You're timing couldn't be better." He gestured with the handkerchief hand. "Perhaps you could attend to Yvette. I am afraid she has had too much to drink... I hope you will forgive us this little scene. The lady is overwrought." He spoke the last to his guests. "Now, if you will excuse me for a moment, I will change my shirt."

With that, as if by silent consensus, the guests turned their backs on Stevens, Luke, Skylar, and Yvette. The volume of voices and laughter slowly rose.

"Get her out of here, Luke. She's your problem now." Stevens pushed the sobbing Yvette straight at Luke, who caught her in his outstretched arms.

"Luke! Oh Luke." Yvette buried her reddened and tear-streaked face against his neck. "I know Martin's through with me now... He will send me away, won't he? I just couldn't stop myself. It was like he didn't even notice I was here... I dressed especially for him. He used to love me in blue. I wanted to get his attention."

"You certainly succeeded," Luke soothed. "Let's get you upstairs. You don't want to make a bad scene worse."

"I have to talk to him, to apologize. Do you think he will ever forgive me?"

"Get her out of here, White," Bill growled.

As Luke led the other girl away, he glanced back at Skylar. She raised her eyebrows questioningly. He nodded to her. Now what was she supposed to make of that gesture, she wondered as he disappeared into the house. She could see he had his hands full, but she didn't understand why attending Escalle's out of control mistress was in his job description.

"Dumb bitch," Bill muttered. "She got margarita all over me, too." He picked up a drink napkin and began to wipe at the sleeves of his gray jacket.

"What happened?"

"Where were you?" Comprehension dawned on the darkly tanned features. "You and White came in together. That guy has always been a smooth operator." He smirked. "Yvette's a crazy bitch, hot, but crazy. The boss has been getting tired of her act for a while now. Tonight, she just lost it when she saw him talking with some other babe. She dumped her drink on him. She should be getting her one-way ticket out of here soon. It's too bad. I wouldn't mind blowing a nut in that one. She wouldn't give me the time of day before, but I don't think she'll be so snooty now."

"So, why did Mr. Escalle dispatch Luke to take care of her?"

"It's his job. Luke cleans things up for the boss."

"What does that entail?"

"You know, things come up." He eyed her lewdly. "You're lookin' fine tonight. Now that Luke is out of the picture, we could have ourselves a good time."

"Thanks, but I'll pass." Skylar started to turn away.

Bill reached out and grabbed her arm. His grip was bruising. "Don't blow me off. I can make things difficult for you around here. I could tell the boss about how I caught you snooping around."

"I wasn't snooping. I was just..."

"Who do you think the boss will believe?"

"Look, Bill. There's no conflict here. It's simply not my style to get involved with two men at the same time. Call me old fashioned. Until I see where things are going with Luke, I'm just not looking for anything else. You can understand that, can't you?"

His grip loosened. "Yeah, I get it. Luke's a loser. He's going nowhere. A smart girl like you should be able to figure that out quick. On the other hand, I have some big plans. You think about it."

"I will, Bill."

She made herself walk slowly away. What a creep. She so wanted to tell him off, but it would have been a dumb move to further antagonize him, rather like waving a red flag in front of an already enraged bull. It was a relief he had accepted her brush-off. For now at least.

* * * *

Skylar was feeling a little slow and dull the following morning. With the aid of a hot shower and some ibuprofen, she managed to appear in a reasonably presentable form at breakfast. Lillian was the only other person at the table. She was nursing a coffee.

"Morning."

"My, aren't you bright eyed and bushy-tailed. I'm old enough now that I pay for my sins of overindulgence."

"Believe me, I'm paying, and you look great."

"You're being kind. I feel a hundred years old."

"Where's Chris?"

"Ms. Connelly, do you want oatmeal again today?" Melanie, a young woman who assisted in the kitchen in the mornings, asked as she poured Skylar a cup of coffee.

"Yes, that would be great… Do you have any of those strawberries left over from yesterday?"

"Yes, we do."

"If it isn't too much trouble, could you throw some of them on the oatmeal?"

"Absolutely. It'll be just a minute."

"Chris," Lillian explained once the kitchen door had swung closed, "is dining with his mother this morning. They are having Belgian waffles in her bed."

"Do you know what time he'll be down?"

"I don't believe Chris will be taking any lessons today. Angelique gave Conny the day off, and you just missed Cole. So, you have the day to yourself. Why don't you do something fun? You haven't seen anything of Key West yet. Be a tourist today. Let your hair down."

"I should work on my thesis." Skylar knew she should work on digging up some more clues on Maia's disappearance. She'd been on Coral Key for a few weeks now, and though she had lots of suspicions, she'd come up with little that was concrete.

"Youth is wasted on the young. If I were your age, and in the Keys, I would be having the time of my life. As a young girl, I must admit, I did enjoy myself. I met Martin, I mean Mr. Escalle, when I was younger than you are now. He was so dashing, so handsome." Lillian lapsed into bemused silence. "It was more than twenty years ago, but it feels like yesterday."

"You've worked for Mr. Escalle since then?"

"I've worked for him for ten years now, but I've known him for twenty. I met him in Annapolis. One of my girlfriends invited me up to the Naval Ball. She set me up with one of her beau's friends, Martin."

"I didn't know Mr. Escalle was a graduate of the Naval Academy."

"He isn't a graduate, but he did attend. Can you keep a secret?"

71

"Scout's honor."

"It was a travesty of a justice really. Martin was thrown out. It was completely unfair, of course."

"What happened?"

"Martin's such a good man. I am sure he must have been taken advantage of. There was a blackmail scandal involving several of the instructors. Martin was blamed. To this day, I believe he knew who was truly responsible, but he wouldn't turn his friends in. He's loyal to a fault. Just think about how generous he has been with poor Angelique.

"Martin didn't approve of his sister marrying Jim Whitfield. Martin and Angelique were estranged for several years afterwards. He didn't think Jim was good enough for his sister. Since Jim's death, Martin has raised Chris as if he were his own, but I shouldn't be airing the family's dirty linen...where was I?"

"Mr. Escalle left the Naval Academy." Skylar prompted.

"Oh yes. I was very taken with him from the moment we met. He went abroad afterwards, to make his fortune. I didn't hear anything from Martin for a long time. Ten years later, we met again. I was working as a personal assistant to a very wealthy octogenarian in Palm Beach. I was no longer the blushing debutante whom he met in Annapolis. You see, my father's business failed, and I had to go to work. Martin remembered me. When my employer passed on, he offered me a job running his household. By then, Angelique was a young lady. He felt she needed a woman's influence."

"Wow, that's quite a story. I don't mean to be nosey," actually, she had every intention of taking advantage of this unusually loquacious mood of Lillian's, "but was there ever a romance between you two? I know I probably shouldn't ask you, but the way you describe Mr. Escalle, why it's like he's your knight in shining armor."

Lillian blushed and tittered. "Oh, he is. There was a time when... Well, it's all ancient history now." She patted a hand to her immaculate French twist, composing herself.

Skylar was now convinced Escalle's housekeeper still harbored a tendre for her employer. "Have you ever been married?"

"Good heavens, no. It isn't that I didn't have opportunities. I had quite a few gentlemen callers, but..."

"None of them quite lit your fire," Skylar offered. "I can understand that. I haven't met anyone I could imagine marrying yet, either." Suddenly, she thought of Luke. She was losing it. The man was definitely not husband material. She could easily imagine spending some mindless nights of passion with him, but not the whole 'I do,' 'until death do us part' routine. He just did not seem like a day-to-day sort of guy.

"You're young yet, dear, and very pretty, too. You won't have any trouble catching a man. Why Bill Stevens was asking me about you last night."

Great, all she needed was that nut coming after her. Time for a change of subject. "I think I just might take your advice and go into Key West today. I've always wanted to visit Hemingway's house. *For Whom the Bell Tolls* and *A Farewell to Arms* have always been two of my favorite books." She also wanted to drop off another roll of film at her safety deposit box. This roll had shots of several more visitors to the house.

"I believe I read them in school, but I don't remember them all that well. I enjoy romance novels myself. Catherine Coulter and Nora Roberts are two of my favorite authors. Have you read any of their books?"

Skylar nodded.

Lillian continued, "Well, if you'll excuse me, I have a number of things I need to get done. Have fun in Key West. It's really quite a unique place. Would you like a picnic lunch? I can have Melanie prepare something for you."

"Oh no. That won't be necessary. I can pick something up on Key West."

* * * *

About twenty minutes later, Skylar sat ready in her Golf. She had her sunglasses on, her purse beside her. She inserted and turned the key. Nothing. The car was dead. She tried again. There wasn't even a clicking sound.

"Shoot," she muttered. She got out, and walked around to the back of the car. She popped the trunk and pulled out the jumper cables. Bessy had her issues. Her odometer had stopped counting at one hundred fifty-thousand plus miles. Admittedly, she'd had some problems with starting, but generally, these occurred when the weather was cold. With the mercury hovering at around eighty-four degrees Fahrenheit, this was definitely not the case. The problem was Bessy hadn't been started in days. She needed a good run, and then she would be fine.

Right now, Skylar had to find someone to jump her car. The parking area was quiet. No one was in sight. She knew where she could probably find Luke, but she wasn't sure she was ready to see him.

Then again, she couldn't deny her heart beat faster at the thought of him.

She walked around the side of the house. As she'd expected, Luke and two other men were at work onboard the *Calypso*. They were so involved in their boat related activities they didn't even notice her approach.

She raised her hand to shield her face from the blindingly bright Florida sun. There was a gentle breeze coming in off the water, which cooled the sweat on her forehead and back. "Hello…? Excuse me, Luke. I don't mean to interrupt you, but I need your help."

"Legs, what can I do for you?" He grinned at her as he casually strolled over. One of the other men, a swarthy, hirsute fellow, leered at her. She resisted the urge to cross her arms defensively. By now, she was used to the fact that Escalle employed some rather unsavory help.

"My car won't start. Could you give me a jump?" She held out the jumper cables to him.

Luke hopped nimbly off the end of the pier and stepped straight up to her. He took the cables in one hand, and took her hand in his other. His grip was firm, warm, and callused. They headed back towards the parking area. Their long-legged strides were smoothly and effortlessly matched.

"Battery dead?"

She shook her head. "The battery should be fine. It's not old. But my car is…"

"Ancient," he supplied. "If it was a horse, I would recommend you take it out and shoot it." He eyed the rusted navy paint of the hood critically. "What's holding this thing together?"

"Bessy got me all the way here from New Hampshire," she countered defensively.

"You've named this heap? You're a beauty. That and the fact you drove this thing all the way to Florida really makes me question your judgment. What if 'Bessy' had broken down on the way? What if you had been stranded? It wasn't a smart thing to do. Escalle would have sent you a plane ticket."

"He offered," she admitted. "I thought I might need a car down here. I'm planning on buying a newer car when I finish my Master's program, Bessy has been a good car." She rested her hand on the top of the Golf. "She gets endless miles to the gallon."

"The boss has several extra cars here. Why don't you take one of them?"

"I couldn't do that."

"Why the hell not? They're here to be used. I'm not suggesting you take one of his personal cars, just one of the extras. Hold on, I'll get you some keys."

She waited while he disappeared into the house. He emerged moments later and tossed her a set of keys.

"Luke, I don't want to inconvenience anyone. Mr. Escalle might be upset if I took one of his cars."

"Do you have a clean driving record?"

"Yes."

"I'm sure Escalle had it checked before you were hired. You're going to have to drive one of his cars if you plan on taking the kid anywhere. Chris told me you were going to take him to the Mel Fisher museum, and there's no way Angelique is going to let him ride in your wreck."

"Bessy is not a wreck."

"Woman, quit arguing. Have you ever driven a Porsche?"

"No... No way. I couldn't."

"Live a little. Take the white Boxter, there. Yvette uses it sometimes, but I don't think she's going anywhere today. If she had plans, she'd be chauffeured. Her driving privileges are done here. She's done here."

Skylar digested this, and considered the white Porsche. It was so sweet. She could just imagine the power under her foot, the smooth acceleration, and best of all, the air conditioning blowing her hair. She swallowed hard. "I'll take it."

"Good girl." Luke wore a surprisingly tender expression. He gripped her shoulders. She closed her eyes, thinking he was going to kiss her, then felt his lips on her forehead. She opened her eyes as he drew back.

"You wanted me to kiss you. Admit it. You thought I was going to lay one on you."

"You really are a jerk, you know that."

"Still, you want me."

She shook her head as she lowered herself into the car. She pulled the door shut, and put the key into the ignition. The performance engine purred to life. She glanced around, located the window controls, and then slid her window down. "Thanks, Luke."

"No problem." He turned away, hesitated, and then stepped back towards the car. "What are you doing tonight?"

"I was just going to check out Key West today, see the sights. I'll probably be back here in the evening sometime."

"I'll be on Duval Street later this afternoon. I have some business to attend to. Want to have dinner with me?"

"That'd be fun."

"Meet me at the Schooner Wharf Bar around eight o'clock."

"Where is this bar?"

"It's right on the Harborwalk. Just ask anyone. It's a landmark."

"Sounds good."

With that, she reversed out of the parking area. She waved at him and grinned. Dinner with Luke promised to be exciting, and she could kill two birds with one stone. She could probe how much he knew about Maia's disappearance, and she could satisfy her own need to gaze into those sensual brown eyes.

The Boxter handled like a dream. The drive was scenic, and varied from tropical exotic to kitschy honky-tonk. Though there was plenty to look at, she found it kind of difficult to stay below fifty-five. She never had this problem with the Golf. She was by no means a speed demon, but the Porsche seemed dissatisfied with the moderate pace. About halfway through her trip, she happened to glance into her rearview mirror. She registered a blue minivan and a black Mustang. About ten minutes later, she observed the minivan was gone, but the Mustang was still behind her.

Another fifteen minutes or so passed, and she saw the black car was still trailing her. Her heart began to pound. Who could be following her? US 1 was the only road straight down through the Keys. The driver of the Mustang was probably heading to Key West, too, she reasoned. She was being paranoid because Maia disappeared, and because she'd made both Luke and Bill suspicious of her. It wasn't like the driver was trying to be subtle or anything. He was two or three car lengths behind her and just hanging out there. In all likelihood, there was no reason for concern.

She refused to glance in her rearview mirror again until she was on Key West. There, the traffic increased dramatically. She pulled over at a convenience store, and heaved a sigh when the black Mustang passed her. She tried to see in the driver's windows, but they were too darkly tinted to make anything out.

She exhaled slowly in relief, and pulled the key out of the ignition. After locking the car up, she headed into the shop. It was full of touristy junk, from postcards of amazing sunsets to seashell decorated boxes, and shot glasses. She purchased a map and a guidebook. Back in the car, she read Hemingway's house was in Old Town Key West. She also learned the entire island was only two miles by four miles. She decided she wanted to walk around, to get a flavor for the place. Therefore, as soon as she was within reasonable distance of the Old Town, she sought out and found a respectable looking, tolled parking area. It was expensive, but she felt more comfortable leaving the Boxter there.

It was a glorious day. The temperature was comfortable, in the high seventies or low eighties with a nice breeze. She studied the map, and headed out. She found herself really enjoying the walk along Duval Street. Even in midmorning, there was plenty to see. The road was an extended strip mall with T-shirt shops, tour shops, art galleries, and funky stores with names like "Condomnation." There were also bars of every type seemingly every few doors.

She bought a bottled water, sat on a bench, and paged through her guidebook. She learned Key West was a wild, fun sort of town with vibrant artist and gay communities. She read the population consisted of an eclectic mix of peoples drawn by the climate, the atmosphere, the fishing, or just because. She enjoyed the people-watching for a while and then set off again.

She turned off Duval into a quiet, stately neighborhood. Magnificent, old Victorian homes draped in lush greenery and tropical flowers resembled ageing Southern beauties in a Tennessee Williams' play. The Old Town area was so fascinating, she was rather disappointed to arrive so quickly at the Hemingway Home and Museum on Whitehead Street.

Once inside the brick wall, which surrounded the place, Skylar was awed by the Spanish Colonial-style house. It was an unusual green shade, which seemed very appropriate for its setting. It was covered in arching windows. Something warm and soft brushed up against her leg. She jumped, then glanced down. A large, fat, multi-colored cat gazed up at her. She reached down to stroke it. She'd read about the many-toed cats that inhabited the house. They were the descendants of Hemingway's own cats.

She joined the flow of tourists, paid her fee, and began to meander through the rooms. She learned Hemingway, or Papa, as he was referred to in the brochures, had lived in the house with his wife Pauline while he was in his early thirties. Many of the furnishings in the house were actually either his or his wife's, and they possessed a comfortable, well-used charm and a delicacy of taste. Even though it was now a museum, the house still felt like a home waiting for its master to return. Skylar lingered in the children's bedroom because she was drawn to its picture of the young Hemingway.

She chuckled at the cat drinking fountain made of an old Spanish olive jar with a urinal base, which came from a Key West bar called 'Sloppy Joe's.' She found herself caught up in this intimate glimpse into a famous author's world. She saved the carriage house for last. Hemingway's studio was housed in its second floor. Now, it was possible to climb a staircase up to the room. In Hemingway's day, the writer had crossed into the smaller building from the main house via a catwalk. There weren't any other tourists up there, so she took her time checking out Hemingway's Royal typewriter and his Cuban cigar-maker's chair. She wondered what books he had written while sitting in this very room, what thoughts he had had while gazing out at a scene, which had remained pretty much unchanged in the years since.

She closed her eyes and imagined Ernest Hemingway walking through the door.

Suddenly, a gunshot rang out. Skylar didn't process what the sound was immediately. She heard someone scream, and the sound of commotion downstairs. She glanced out the window, toward the house.

Another shot shattered a windowpane just beside her.

Chapter Nine

She hit the deck, and began to crawl toward the stairs. Someone was definitely shooting, and possibly shooting at her.

She scrambled down the steps. The first floor was chaotic.

"What's happening? What's going on?" she demanded of a panicked-looking older woman who wore a nametag.

"Someone was shooting a gun! My Lord. I can't believe this."

Skylar glanced around. Tourists were rushing for the exit, and the Hemingway House staff clearly didn't have a handle on the situation.

She hurried into the bookstore. "Excuse me," she called out to a thin, young man who was involved in an animated conversation on his phone.

"Hemingway House. All right. We'll try to keep everyone here." He hung up, held up a finger to indicate she should wait, and then punched in a few numbers on his phone. "Yes. Hello. This is Timothy at the Bookstore. The police are on their way. No one is to leave the grounds. No exceptions... All right." He hung up.

"The police are coming," she repeated. "I think they were shooting at me. I was up in the studio. They shot right through the window!"

"Isn't it horrible," Timothy remarked, though his expression revealed a very different emotion. "You can't leave now. No one can. At least the place isn't too busy yet. I wonder if the shooter is still out there?" The idea was obviously strangely appealing to him.

Skylar exchanged a few more words with Timothy, and then headed out toward the gate to wait for the police. There she found two security guards attempting to convince a group of ladies of mature years to stay put. In minutes, she heard sirens, and then Key West's finest pulled up.

She was one of the first people to be interviewed, and she led the rather stout, crew cut, forty-something cop back up to the studio.

"Here. I was standing right here. I was looking out the window. I didn't recognize that the first shot was a gunshot. I've never heard a real gun, just TV guns."

"You heard the gun shot, Ms. Donnelly?"

"Connelly," she corrected automatically.

"You stuck your head by the window to see who was shooting at what, and then there was this other shot?"

"See, it took out the window pane."

"Yes, I've got it. Thanks for showing me, Ms. Connelly. You have anything else you want to tell me?"

"That's it."

"We'll call you to come down and sign your statement when we get it typed up." He turned to head back down the stairs.

"Aren't you going to do something about this?" She gestured at the windowpane.

"Ms. Connelly, the ballistics guys are on their way. I don't want to mess up any evidence, and I've got to get some more statements. There's a right way of doing things. We'll take care of it."

"Officer Nelson," she took a deep breath. "I think the shooter may have been aiming for me."

He paused and turned to face her. "Miss, I think that's highly unlikely. It was probably just some kid with a BB gun."

"I heard real gun shots. Everyone did."

"Nowadays, those things are made to sound realistic. My boy has one. Scared the bejeesus out of me the first time he fired it. Don't worry. We'll get to the bottom of this."

"Officer Nelson, I am not a paranoid person. I don't know how to say this, but I think someone followed me here, and then shot at me."

"Do things like this happen to you often, Ms. Connelly?" Now there was a wary look to his eyes.

"No. Never. I'm not crazy. There was this black Mustang on the road coming into Key West, and I swear it was following me."

"Did you get a license plate number?"

"No, it was behind me. I didn't think to look at it."

"How long did it follow you?" He wore the expression of one

jumping through the expected hoops. His voice sounded disinterested.

"Twenty minutes or so. I'm not paranoid."

"I'll put it in your statement."

In frustration, Skylar glanced around the studio and noticed the hole.

"Wait. There! Do you see it? The bullet's right there."

Nelson's expression morphed from lazy disinterest to real absorption. About an hour later, Skylar accompanied Nelson, and his partner, a silver-haired giant named Officer Behling, to the police station. There, the officers went over her account again and asked her some questions. Finally, a few hours later, she was allowed to leave the station. Just before departing, she approached Officer Behling: "If you find out anything, will you call me?"

"We'll be in touch."

"That doesn't mean you'll tell me anything, does it?"

"No, it doesn't. We can't jeopardize an active investigation by releasing classified information. At the moment, we don't have a suspect or even a profile of one. If for any reason we suspect your safety is at risk, we'll let you know." The man had tired hazel eyes, and a long, drooping mustache. "We're collecting evidence as we speak. It'll probably be a couple of days before our guys come up with anything definitive. Thanks for being so cooperative." He glanced back down at a form he was filling out.

"What if this guy tries to shoot me again?"

Behling paused in his writing. He looked at her. "You got any reason for someone to take shots at you? Maybe a pissed off old boyfriend?"

"No, of course not." The denial rang hollow in her ears. "I just…want to be safe."

"It's our job to keep you safe. There's probably no safer place for you in the Keys than at Casa del Mar. Mr. Escalle has really top security people. I know because I was an advisor on some of the security measures installed at the estate. You'll be just fine there."

She bit her lip. Escalle had really done a job on the Key West police force. Officer Behling considered him a pillar of the community. She decided not to share her suspicions regarding her employer. She didn't believe she would be taken seriously.

She wondered if this man had handled Maia's case. If Behling's attitude concerning Escalle was characteristic of the rest of the police force, it was not surprising her sister's disappearance had been handled so perfunctorily, as it must have been a cause for some discomfort to Escalle.

"Thank you, officer. Well, if we're done here, I should get going. I have an engagement this evening."

"You mean a date, don't ya? That's what we used to call 'em. Yup, we're all done here. You can go."

She nearly ground her teeth as she left the office. Without spilling the proverbial beans, there was no way she could convince them she was in danger, and she didn't want to risk not being allowed to return to Casa del Mar.

Skylar decided she would start an e-mail log on her computer. She would update it each day, and forward it as an attachment to Laura with the instructions to open it only if something happened to her. Skylar also decided that when the time came to bring in law enforcement professionals, she was not going to waste her time with the local authorities.

She checked her watch as she slipped behind the steering wheel of the Porsche. It was already three-forty. That didn't give her enough time to drive back, shower, change, and then return to Key West. There was no way she was going to miss out on her evening with Luke White. There were too many important questions she wanted to put to him. Being shot at and then summarily dismissed as a paranoid nut had effectively worn through her patience. She wanted some answers. She believed she stood a better chance of getting answers by facing Luke in a 'safe' setting, one in which neither one of them were at an advantage.

She debated blowing the next two hours by doing some more sightseeing, and then meeting Luke as she was. Key West appeared to be a rather casual town, but she dismissed this plan.

Skylar used the keyless entry device to unlock the Porsche. Inside the car, the air was hot and stale, and the black leather upholstery was uncomfortably warm and sticky against the backs of her thighs. After looking around in vain for a cloth of some sort, she wiggled her shorts down as low as she could to protect her skin. She cranked up the air conditioner and turned the temp down. Almost instantly, a front of cold air blasted out at her.

Calypso's Secrets

* * * *

As Skylar headed round a bend on the Harborwalk, steamy and vibrant Reggae tones spilled out of the building she was nearing. The warm day had faded to a comfortable evening. There was just enough breeze coming off the water to cool her skin and to play with the fine hairs along her hairline. She'd located the Schooner Wharf Bar easily. While shopping at a dress boutique, she simply asked.

A Christie Brinkley look-alike sold her the clingy, multicolored mini-dress she was currently wearing. The girl assured her the dress was "*so-o* Key West," and she "had to flaunt her legs, since they were *cut*."

With the girl standing there, singing her praises, Skylar had been sure this was the right dress for the evening. She had felt apprehensive when she slipped the scrap of fabric on after rinsing off at a beach side shower. She put her makeup on in the Boxter's driver's side mirror. As for her hair, she left it down and allowed it to dry into a wild, gypsy-like mane.

Judging from the catcalls and whistles she evoked while walking towards her destination, Skylar was reassured she looked pretty good. By the time she was seated at a round table on the second floor deck of the Schooner Wharf Bar sipping an ice-cold beer and gazing out at the magnificent yachts in the harbor, she was feeling decidedly better.

"Skylar, you out slumming tonight?"

She looked up to find Bill Stevens leering at her. He continued to eye her lasciviously as he took a seat at her table.

"I'm expecting someone."

"You work fast." The no-necked bodyguard was wearing a skintight, black T-shirt that almost cut into his rounded biceps. She wondered where he had secreted the gun he always wore, since he obviously couldn't fit a shoulder holster under his shirt.

As he grinned at her, she could make out the acne scars carved into his five o'clock shadow, and his horsy front teeth had a gray cast to them. She wondered idly how many times they had been knocked out.

"What can I do for you, Bill?"

"I can think of a couple of things, and I usually prefer blondes with bigger tits, but I could make an exception for you."

"If this is just a social call..."

"Hey, I'm here to do you a favor." He held up his hands innocently opened.

"What do you mean?"

"You and White. You're doing him, right?"

"It's really none of your business." She glared at the Neanderthal opposite her.

"Seriously, White may seem like an easy going guy, and he definitely has a way with the ladies, but you should watch yourself around him."

"What do you mean by that?"

"He's not someone you wanna cross."

"I'm really not interested in your thoughts on Luke."

"Take it or leave it, I'm just giving you fair warning."

"Why on earth do you think I would place any merit in your opinion of Luke?"

"I know the guy. I've worked with him a while."

She pushed her chair back. "I'm not interested in hearing any more. Luke's joining me this evening. If you won't leave this table, I will."

"I'd guessed you were meeting up with him. Listen to me, there was this other chick, she was working with the brat, too. She started looking into things that weren't her business. The boss was getting kind of concerned about her. He told Luke to handle the situation. The girl disappeared the next day."

A surge of fear and adrenalin shot through her. "Are you telling me Mr. Escalle told Luke to do something to this girl?"

"You've been sniffing around the place, too, like that other girl. People have noticed. Now, White's all over you. Have I painted the picture for you?"

"Is Escalle doing anything illegal?"

Stevens peered around to make sure no one was close by them. Speaking *sotto voce*, he continued: "I've told you all I can. Bottom line, the girl's gone, and I mean in a big way. I'm betting her body will wash up on shore one day, if the sharks leave anything."

Skylar struggled to quash the wave of horror that swept through her. She closed her eyes, trying to block out the image Stevens just described. She had to believe Maia was still alive, and she would keep hoping and praying until the facts proved otherwise.

"Why are you telling me this? You expect me to believe you are some sort of white knight?"

"I know you think I'm a bad-ass, but I'm not into killin' chicks. I can stomach Escalle. He pays well, and I like the work, but White is dangerous."

"You think Escalle ordered Luke to kill this girl?" Disbelief laced her tone with scorn.

"No, Escalle told White to call her off. Luke was the one who offed her. He's a killer."

"If you honestly believe all of this, why haven't you told Escalle?"

"The boss needs someone like him. But I'm watching him. I don't want any of his shit smearing the boss."

She was silent for a moment. "How did you know I was here this evening?"

"I came on a hunch. Lillian told me you came into town. This bar's Luke's favorite place. Then, I saw the Porsche in the lot."

"Have you been in Key West all day?" She observed the bodyguard carefully, wondering whether he would betray any knowledge of the shots fired at the Hemingway house.

"I had to see some people."

"May I join the party?" Luke interrupted smoothly as he drew back a chair.

She glanced up at him in frustration and confusion. She wanted to hear Bill's alibi, and she had no idea of how to interact with Luke now. She'd just been told Luke killed Maia. And now, he was here, looking relaxed and sexy. He wore tan cargo pants with a short-sleeved, gray-green shirt, which was unbuttoned lower than she was used to seeing. The scent of Hugo drifted around him, mixing with his warm, salty masculinity. A diamond stud twinkled in one ear. To her shame, her body reacted to him instantly, despite what she had been told.

"White, I was just leaving." Bill stood up.

"Bill, you making a move on my girl?" Luke grinned, but Skylar caught the intensity of the looks exchanged between the two men.

"Trying to, but she shot me down."

"Good girl."

"Think about what I said, Skylar. Try the rumrunners." They watched as Bill swaggered through the restaurant. He headed straight for the exit, angling himself sideways when his massively muscled shoulders were too broad for him to pass straight through an area.

"What was that all about?"

"I'm not really sure," she shrugged.

"Don't have anything to do with Bill. He's bad news... But I don't intend to let him ruin our evening. You look sensational tonight. I like your hair down like that. It's really sexy."

She resisted the urge to pull her heavy, dark mane over to one side of her neck. She also fought the blush rising in her cheeks. She had to stay focused. "Funny, Stevens said the same the thing about you."

"He thinks I'm sexy?"

"No, he thinks you're dangerous." Impulsively, she decided to grab the bull by the horns. "He says you had something to do with the disappearance of a girl, one who worked for Escalle."

To her amazement, he didn't look horrified or even defensive. In fact, he chuckled. "I didn't think old Bill was smart enough to figure that one out."

She felt sick to the stomach. Was it possible this man to whom she was so attracted was her sister's murderer?

Chapter Ten

Skylar stared at Luke. "What do you mean? What did you do to this girl?"

"Nothing really. I merely pointed out it would be in her best interest to seek employment elsewhere."

"So, she left. That's it?"

"Yup. Despite the impression that Bullet Bill gave you, there's nothing sinister to the story."

"She just packed up and went home?"

"Yes." His expression remained calm and relaxed. But she knew he was lying to her.

"Hello, my name is Jolene," a very tanned young woman tapped her nametag. "I'll be your waitress. Can I get you anything to drink?"

"Skylar," he prompted. "What would you like to have? I'm going to have a beer."

"Fine," she muttered, distracted by her thoughts and worries.

"Do you want to have a beer?"

She nodded, and held up her now empty glass. "MGD, please," she directed the waitress.

The facts were obvious, though she wanted to scream in pain and anger at her new knowledge. Luke had been involved in Maia's disappearance; she felt it, in her bones.

"We'll have a pitcher of MGD... Skylar, do you trust me to order for us? I know the menu here pretty well."

"Go ahead."

"We'll start with conch fritters and buffalo wings. What's the catch of the day?" he asked the waitress.

"Mahi Mahi."

"We'll have that," he nodded and finished the order.

Skylar waited to speak until the waitress was out of listening range. "Why did you tell this girl to leave?"

"She's putting our order in."

"Not the waitress, the girl who…left. Bill made it all sound so sinister."

"Her name was Maia. Conny came down with shingles last summer. So this girl was hired to help with Chris until Conny got back on her feet. She was a nice kid."

"And? What happened?"

He eyed her intently. "Let's just drop the whole subject. I was looking forward to a pleasant evening with you, not an interrogation about some girl I barely knew. Don't let Bill spoil things for us. You're playing right into his hands."

"Here's your beer." Jolene dropped off a large pitcher and two ice-cold glasses.

Luke expertly poured for both of them. He handed Skylar a glass. Then he reached across the table and took her hand.

"What's going on here, Skylar?"

"You're not telling me the truth about this Maia, are you?"

"If you're asking if there was anything going on between us, there wasn't. She was cute and well put together, but a kid. She and Cole were seeing each other for a while. She ended up taking off with some other guy. The whole thing was no big deal."

"Bill really pulled a number on you, didn't he. So much for my plans for the evening."

"Luke, where were you this afternoon?" She was relieved to see he didn't appear at all uncomfortable with this question.

"I worked on the yacht for most of the day. Then, I showered, changed, and headed into town. On the way, I stopped and visited with an old buddy. That's why I was a couple of minutes late. Why this sudden curiosity?"

She decided this was not the time to hold back. The whole situation was quickly becoming downright perilous. "Someone shot at me today."

"What?" He looked both surprised and shocked. "When did this happen?"

"This morning at the Hemingway house. I was up in the study, and someone took a shot at me. Or, actually, two shots."

"Are you all right?"

"Yes, I'm fine. They missed. I'm just a little shaken up."

"You should be… Skylar, I think you have to take this as a warning. Someone is telling you to back off. We both know you have taken a less than healthy interest in Escalle's affairs. My guess is the shooter missed you deliberately, to scare you off."

"Luke, tell me what's going on at Casa del Mar."

He considered for a moment. "You're an amateur, Skylar. This game isn't for you."

She now knew it was likely he had been involved in Maia's disappearance, but she still didn't believe he was a killer. She took a deep breath, and then plunged impetuously on. "You're a gun runner, aren't you? For Escalle. I thought he was dealing drugs at first, and I still think that's a possibility… That's what this is all about, isn't it?"

"Keep your voice down, Skylar. How did you? Never mind. You've got to leave the Keys."

"What happened to Maia?" she persisted.

He leaned closer. Now, the casual languor that generally characterized his movements was gone, replaced by an electric intensity. "You're playing with fire, and you're going to get burned. Take my advice, and get out of here."

"Why? Explain to me why I have to go."

"Wake up, Skylar. Someone's using you for target practice. Besides, what's keeping you here?"

"What do you do for Escalle? What's his hold on you?"

"We are talking about some seriously bad guys. I don't want you to get caught in the crossfire."

"I can look out for myself."

"You did a fine job of that today."

"I'll go to the FBI."

"Escalle's business falls under the ATF's jurisdiction. They're the ones you should go to with any information you've unearthed. I wouldn't bother with the local police. Escalle has really done a job on them. They genuinely believe he's a solid citizen."

"I saw that today. You're telling me to go to the authorities?" Surprise and disbelief rang clearly in her voice. "Why? You work for him, don't you? I don't understand."

"I wish I could explain it all to you, but doing so would place you in greater danger. I won't do that to you."

"Aren't you being a little melodramatic? It's not like Escalle is going to shoot me full of truth serum."

"Someone shot at you today," he calmly pointed out. "There are other people involved here, people who have already sacrificed a great deal."

"Are you some kind of agent or cop?"

"You're just going to have to trust me, Skylar. If it were up to me, I'd tell you everything you want to know."

"Why should I trust you? You could be lying to me right now."

"You haven't exactly been honest and straight forward yourself." His expression softened. "I wish circumstances were different, that I had met you at some other place, at some other time. Hell, at any other time. Then, I'd want to ask you…" He paused as if unsure of how to proceed.

"You'd want to ask me what?"

"Conch fritters and buffalo wings. Here are some extra plates. Can I get you two anything else?" The waitress' arrival shattered the moment. Both Skylar and Luke glanced up at her, and away from each other.

"No, we're fine. Thanks," Luke said.

As if by mutual consent, for the rest of the evening, the two discussed only mundane matters. Initially, Skylar was tense and anxious as a result of her discussions with Bill and Luke. Her mind was spinning, but Luke didn't allow their conversation to grow stilted and awkward. He recounted amusing stories and anecdotes about the Florida Keys and their inhabitants. As the evening progressed, she found herself relaxing and enjoying herself. Luke was a genuinely entertaining companion, and he was applying himself to being charming and witty. In addition, the food was excellent.

A few hours later, they strolled arm-in-arm back to where she parked the Porsche. Skylar considered the evening's revelations. Despite all Luke said, not said, and asked of her, something inside her still trusted him. She usually had a good nose for people, and even now, she doubted that she could be so wrong about someone.

"Well, thanks for dinner. It was delicious." She reached down to open the car door.

"What's your hurry?" He placed his hands on her hips, and maneuvered her up against the side of the car. "You know, we could ride back together. Take the leap, sweetheart. Trust me."

"I'd like to, but I don't feel comfortable leaving this car here." In addition, she needed time to process all he'd told her, to examine her feelings.

"We could leave my jeep." He reached out and stroked a long strand of hair back behind her ear.

She shivered. He drew her closer, up against his firm warmth.

"Luke, we don't... Neither of us..."

"*Shh.*" He touched his fingertips to her lips. "I know. I know." His lips softly brushed hers. Closing her eyes, she leaned into him. She savored how feminine she felt pressed against his long, hard length. She inhaled the rich, masculine scent of his cologne.

Abruptly, he stepped back away from her. He grinned at her when she opened her eyes in some confusion. "I'll take a rain check then, doll. See you at the house."

"Aren't you even disappointed?" She was chagrinned at how easily he switched gear.

"Sure, I am. Some things are meant to be. You and I are going to happen. So, I'm not going to sweat the fact it won't be tonight. I plan to enjoy the anticipation. I'll go to sleep dreaming of you, and if I can't sleep, well then I'll tug a batch thinking of you."

She couldn't help herself. She burst out laughing at the outrageous comment. The guy was completely irreverent and wholly uninhibited.

He performed a jaunty salute, then strolled away. Just before he disappeared from her view, she heard him begin to whistle a tune.

It was only once she was safely ensconced in the car that the magic spell his charm had woven began to wear off. It dawned on her he hadn't really answered any of her questions concerning Maia. Instead, he had romanced her away from the subject.

Luke was too much of an unknown quantity. She had no good reason to believe in him. What other alternative did she have? Was she crazy for being attracted to a man who in all likelihood had something to do with her sister's disappearance? She gripped the steering wheel in frustration. She shoved her hair back behind her ear and started the engine. It was going to be a long ride home.

* * * *

About an hour later, Skylar arrived at the gates of Casa del Mar. The drive had been soothing and peaceful, and she listened to country music all the way, singing loudly. Feeling loose and relaxed as she made the final turn, coming upon a police car with flashing lights parked beside the entrance to the opened gates was a complete shock to her.

"What the heck?" She slowed to a stop.

A young, black, very fit looking police officer stepped in front of her car and up to her door.

"What's going on?" She asked.

"Police business. Your name, please?"

"My name is Skylar Connelly. I work here."

"Just a minute." He grabbed a cell phone off his utility belt and dialed a number.

"Yes sir. Connelly… Skylar. Yes sir." He replaced his phone. Then, he leaned down to address her. "You may proceed to the house. An officer will direct you from there."

"What's happened?"

"I'm not at liberty to discuss it. The officers in the house will fill you in on what you need to know."

"All right." She felt very uneasy as she progressed down the lane. Inside the compound, she became even more alarmed. There were at least four police cars parked right in front of the house. She drove around to the parking area, and there she encountered another policeman.

"Ms. Connelly?"

"Yes?"

"Please return to the house by way of the front door. Someone should soon be available to take your statement."

"Oh, this is about the shooting. There's been some misunderstanding. I already gave my statement at the police station. I spoke with an Officer Behling."

He frowned. "We are investigating a potential homicide, but there have been no reports of a gun being involved."

"Homicide?" The fear churned in her stomach. "Who?"

Chapter Eleven

The policeman nodded. "They're ready for you, Ms. Connelly."

With each step, Skylar's heart beat faster as she walked through the now brightly lit parking area. She noticed Luke's jeep was in its usual spot. *Don't let it be Luke. Let him be all right. Please, God.* She chanted the litany all the way to the house.

She wanted everyone else to be okay, too, and she knew it was selfish to think only of him. *But please God, let him be alive.*

A policewoman opened the front door for her.

"Ms. Connelly?"

"Yes."

"This way." She led her through the entrance foyer and into the living room. Angelique, Lillian, and Cole were already seated there. Both women were wearing bathrobes. Lillian's was a pale green terry cloth, and Angelique wore a frothy apricot confection. Cole was dressed in a gray sweat suit.

"Oh, Skylar, thank goodness you are all right." Lillian rushed over to her and grasped her hands. "Can you believe this has happened? I always knew…the girl was unstable."

"What's happened?" She wondered where Luke was.

"Yvette's dead." Angelique announced from where she sat on one of the arms of the couch.

"What?"

"Ladies, please. I would appreciate the opportunity to speak with Ms. Connelly." The policewoman touched Skylar on the shoulder, indicating she was ready to proceed immediately.

Skylar was willing to follow, but Lillian was clinging to her. The older woman was very distraught. She wasn't sure how to disentangle herself. "Lillian, I um." Then, to her surprise, Angelique came up and drew Lillian to her. Lillian, though taller and broader, collapsed into her arms.

Skylar followed the officer into the dining room and both women sat down.

"I've been in touch with Officer Behling regarding the events which took place earlier today at the Hemingway house. As a result, we have a full account of your activities through the early afternoon. Please tell me where you were and what you did between the time you left the police station and when you met up with—" She glanced down to check the notes in her notebook—"Bill Stevens and Luke White at the Schooner Wharf Bar?"

"I didn't have enough time to come home, change, and then get back to Key West in time for my date with Luke. So I bought a dress at a boutique on Duval Street. I have the receipt in my purse. Then, I rinsed off at a beach shower, changed, and then walked along Duval until it was time for my date." Skylar reached down and rifled through her purse. "I know I have it somewhere. Here, here it is. The shop was called the Blue Iguana. A young blond woman helped me. I don't remember her name. I was in there for about half an hour."

The policewoman diligently took notes. She was still looking down at her notebook when she asked her next question. "Are you romantically involved with both Luke White and Bill Stevens?"

"What? What does that have to do with anything?"

"I don't mean to be intrusive. I'm attempting to determine where your loyalties lie. It's not a frivolous question as you are important to both of their alibis."

"Oh, I see. I don't even like Bill Stevens. Luke and I...I'm not sure what we have going on. But I would say we are involved."

"You went out with both men this evening?"

"I had plans to meet with Luke. Bill Stevens showed up before Luke got there. He just came up to my table and sat down."

"Do you remember what time he arrived?"

"I was supposed to meet with Luke at eight. He was about fifteen minutes late. I'd guess Bill got there ten minutes before Luke."

"That puts him there at five after eight."

"Yes, but I don't know how long he was at the bar before he came up to me."

In her mind's eye, Skylar pictured the vehicle she thought followed her into Key West, but she decided not to say anything. Her concerns were already on record with the police. Besides if Stevens was driving that car and was, therefore, away from Casa del Mar during the time period in question, she worried drawing attention to the point would cast more suspicion on Luke, who had spent most of the day at the house.

"Why were you driving the car Yvette Dunbar generally used?"

"My own wouldn't start. It was my understanding Yvette was no longer supposed to drive the Porsche. Luke told me to go ahead and use the car, Mr. Escalle wouldn't mind."

"Can you tell me about last night's party and about Ms. Dunbar's behavior?"

Skylar acquiesced, relating the details of all she had observed.

When she was finished, the police officer stood up. "Thank you, Ms. Connelly. We'll let you know if we have any more questions. You're welcome to rejoin the others."

"Can I ask you...? I don't mean to be morbid, but how was Yvette killed?"

"We aren't sure it was a homicide. Yvette Dunbar appears to have died as the result of an overdose of her own prescription medications. We'll have to wait for the report from the medical examiner to be sure."

Skylar walked back to the living room in something of a daze. Yvette was dead. Just like that, she was gone. It seemed so unreal. In the living room, she exchanged platitudes with Angelique, Lillian, and Cole. The atmosphere remained strained and awkward. It was a great relief when they were permitted to retire for the night.

Over the next few days, the mood at Casa del Mar was subdued. The coroner's report corroborated the theory Yvette died of an overdose of Oxycontin. Apparently, the model had become addicted to the medication following her breast enhancement surgery. Her death was ruled accidental.

There was a brief stir in the local papers. Yvette had been a relatively well-known model, and she and Escalle appeared with some frequency in the society pages, but the house remained strangely quiet in the wake of the death. The security measures employed at the compound kept the reporters and photographers at bay. For the most part, the inhabitants of the house didn't venture out much. Even Angelique curtailed her usual round of charitable activities. Luke was the only member of the household who didn't behave according to this pattern. He continued to make his almost nightly trips out in the *Calypso*.

* * * *

About two weeks after Yvette's death, there was a knock at Skylar's bedroom door. She had just gotten out of the shower following her morning swim.

"Just a minute. I'm not decent." She wrapped the thick, fluffy, pale blue bath towel around her body and stepped back into the bedroom with the intention of donning her bathrobe.

The door swung open, and Luke strolled in. His stared at her, taking in the total picture, from the top of her wet head, down the toned curves of her shoulders, over the lush tops of her breasts, along her wet legs to her feet. His gaze lingered on her toenails, which were painted a sparkly peach.

"I'd say you're much better than decent." He stepped up to her and gently tucked the loose end of her towel down between her breasts.

She swallowed hard. It wasn't fair. He could turn her insides to mush with only a look or a touch.

He chuckled. His brown eyes were intense, though his expression remained deliberately casual. "Sweet thing, I hope I don't run into anyone on my way back downstairs. All of that honey colored skin of yours. It makes me want to lick you all over." He ran a fingertip along the sensitive and vulnerable arch of her collarbone.

Emboldened by her near nudity and his obviously enthusiastic response to it, she raised one dark eyebrow at him. "Luke, you're teasing me."

Boldly, he placed his hands on her hips and pulled her full up against him.

"You're going to get all wet."

"Not as wet as I'm going to make you." Then, he was kissing her in that mind-draining, intoxicating way of his. She was vaguely aware that his hands had drifted down to her bottom. He slid his warm, callused palms underneath the towel, and onto her butt. There, he kneaded and caressed her.

Her hands worked their way up his back. She felt the towel come loose between them, against his chest.

"*Sky-lar... Sky-lar*, you ready yet?" It was Chris. Lately, it had become his practice to accompany her downstairs for breakfast.

They broke apart instantly. Luke was with it enough to catch the edge of her towel and re-tuck it before the boy came into view.

Skylar squashed the urge to touch her lips as Chris appeared in the doorway.

"Oh, you're not ready yet. Hey, Luke. What are you doing up here?"

"I was telling Skylar about a barracuda I saw out on the reef."

"Really? That's so cool. Did you get a picture of it?"

"Not this time, champ."

"Too bad."

The two adults exchanged a relieved look. Chris was young enough and innocent enough to be easily distracted from the problematic issue of Luke being in a nearly naked Skylar's bedroom.

"Skylar, please hurry up. Tyler is going to be here soon, and we're having eggs benedict today. It's my favorite."

"It's one of my favorites, too. I'll be just a minute, Chris." She picked up the shorts, T-shirt, and undergarments she had set out on the vanity chair before her shower and darted back into the privacy and safety of the bathroom.

From the other side of the door, she heard Chris ask, "How come you're all wet, Luke?"

She winced. The kid was observant.

"Oh, it must have happened while I was working on the *Calypso*."

"Skylar says I'm swimming better each day. Maybe I'll swim in the ocean one day."

"I know you will, champ. When you're ready, I'll take you snorkeling on the reef."

"Really? Do you think I could do it?"

"I know you could."

Skylar caught herself smiling into the mirror. "Idiot." She muttered.

So the guy liked kids, too. That didn't prove he wasn't a murderer or at least a criminal, but her gut insisted he was one of the good guys.

In a few minutes, she was ready to go. "All right, men. Let's not keep the eggs benedict waiting."

* * * *

The morning passed pleasantly enough, but by afternoon, Skylar was feeling tense and frustrated. Chris was off with Cole, so there were no specific demands on her time. She had nothing to read. In fact, she realized she had nothing worthwhile to do. She was very aware that time was passing, and she wasn't getting very far in her investigation into Maia's disappearance.

She had the definite sense something important was in the works. Escalle, Luke, and Bill had been busy and preoccupied. Twice in the past week alone, men had arrived at the Coral Key estate, met with Escalle, and then departed. She was sure these weren't casual guests, for the men had interacted only with Escalle and his lieutenants. They were never even introduced to the rest of the family.

Her wheels spinning, she paced the blue room. She peered out the window. There were no cars either coming or going. The estate was as still, humid, and quiet as the very air.

She realized she was chewing on her thumbnail and stopped in disgust. Nail biting was a nervous habit she'd struggled with since her childhood. She had to keep it together, for Maia.

The thought of her sister drew her to sit down at the little writing desk. She flipped on the power on her laptop. She waited a moment, then clicked onto the Internet connection. She selected e-mail. There were no new messages in her Hotmail account.

Idly, she clicked on her inbox. She slid back through time, through old messages to the final one from 'hotteacher.' Maia had sent it to her in July of last summer. Skylar read through it. In it, Maia related she'd met two guys, one of whom was obviously Cole, and the other she described as "kind of a bad boy." She related her concerns that Escalle was involved in illegal activities, and that she'd seen men loading crates onto the *Calypso* late at night. Maia had ended her e-mail promising to go to the police in the near future.

It was the last Skylar heard from her sister. On the very next evening their mother received a call from Martin Escalle. Maia had apparently abandoned her position to run off with a man.

Skylar didn't believe the story for even a second. She knew Maia had snuck onto the *Calypso*, and she guessed she was caught, but by whom? By Escalle? By Bill Stevens? Or, though she hated considering the possibility, had Luke discovered Maia aboard the yacht, and then disposed of her somehow?

She propped the tips of her fingers against each other, and stared out of the window, considering all of the possibilities. She didn't want to suspect Luke, but she couldn't completely rule him out either. She concluded it was all very depressing and confusing when she happened to glimpse a jogger heading around the side of the house. She rose to her feet and, peering out the window, she followed his progress and recognized Cole as the jogger. He was heading into a section of the guesthouse that had been converted into a gym.

She had to admit, he was very fit, with a lean runner's build. She could easily imagine her sister being attracted to this cerebral athlete.

Skylar preferred more substantial, *menschy* men, with broad shoulders and well-muscled thighs, who had no problem hefting her hundred and forty pounds.

Men like Luke White...

She forced herself to stop following this train of thought as the door closed behind Cole. She realized she'd never really investigated him. She'd been too caught up in thinking about the more obvious suspects.

Then again, the fact she'd found Maia's picture in his bedroom was one of the primary reasons she'd let him off the hook in her own mind. After all, you didn't display a picture of someone in your room unless you cared about them. Still, there was a chance she could learn something from him, and she wasn't in a position to disregard any potential leads.

She hurried to her dresser and rifled through the drawers, searching for her work out gear. She quickly located a sports bra, tank top, and running shorts. She decided she could use a little weight work, as well as an opportunity to talk with Cole alone.

After tying the laces on her tennis shoes, she rushed over to the guesthouse. It was a good-sized stucco building which echoed the main house in design and decoration. The entire first floor of the building was devoted to a work out area. The second floor was split into two apartments, in one of which, she knew, Luke lived. She had every intention of getting into those apartments one day and looking around.

She'd been shown the gym upon arrival. She'd considered working out there once or twice, but the lure of the open water had overcome any impulse she'd had to pump iron, and Chris was too young for weight training.

She swung open the door on a very complete gym, which boasted a wall of windows on one side that offered an amazing view of the azure water glistening in the sunlight. The room fairly shook with the music of the Violent Femmes. Skylar recognized the band even though she didn't particularly care for them. Maia had always loved the Femmes.

Skylar heard the heavy metallic clank of weights being released over the throbbing music.

"Hey, Cole," she shouted. "You mind if I join you?"

"What?" He appeared different than he usually did. His blond hair looked darker, wet and slicked back with sweat and water, and his face was ruddy with exertion. She watched as a drop of moisture slid over a hard, flat pectoral muscle. A line of auburn hair traced its way down his belly and into his running shorts. He had a towel draped around his neck, and he looked both aloof and annoyed at the interruption.

"Would you turn down the music?" she shouted.

"What?"

"Turn down the music." She mimed turning a knob.

He nodded understanding, and turned to adjust the boom box sitting on the floor behind him. Then, he stood and faced her, his hands gripping either end of his towel.

She smiled. "You mind if I join you?"

"Help yourself. I'm almost done. I just want to do a few more sets on the bench."

"If I'm bothering you, I can come back."

"No. No, really, it's no problem at all. Please excuse my abruptness. I'm in a zone after I run. I didn't mean to be rude."

"You weren't. This place is amazing."

"Yes, it really is a very complete facility. As you can see, we have quite a lot of cardio equipment, an array of Nautilus machines, and free weights, too. There are even saunas and hot tubs off of each dressing room."

"Wow. I had no idea. Is Mr. Escalle into working out?"

He shook his head. His slight smile offered her a glimpse of the kind of perfectly aligned white teeth only good orthodontia can produce. "Actually, I think I'm the only one who ever uses this place during the day. Luke works out at night. I tried to talk him into training with me, but he's not a morning person, and I do generally work out early in the day."

"That's too bad. I generally prefer to work out with someone else, particularly when I'm doing weights. I push myself harder than when I train alone."

"I am pretty self-motivated, but I could use a spotter sometimes."

"I'd volunteer, but I don't think I could help you with the kind of weight you're benching."

"You might be surprised. I'm kind of wimpy on the upper body."

She wandered over to a treadmill, which looked out over the water. She turned the machine on, and began a warm up walk. "Do you like the Keys?"

Cole finished taking a drink of water before answering her. "I don't particularly care for how touristy the islands are, but I do find them beautiful. Miami is more my cup of tea."

"How long have you worked down here?"

"For a little more than a year. I came down here last spring. I've finished all of the course work for my PhD, and, like you, I'm working on a draft of my thesis."

"How's it coming?"

"I have had it mostly finished for some time. I send it off to my advisor periodically, and he returns it with suggestions for revisions. To be honest, I'm in no hurry to get it finished."

"I'm surprised to hear you say that. Everyone I know who has ever worked on a thesis, including myself, is almost desperate to get it done and approved."

"I wanted to get away from an academic environment in order to assess where I was and where I was going. I needed to do something altogether different. So, here I am."

"I don't mean to be intrusive, Cole, but will you go back when Chris leaves for school?"

He rubbed his eyes with his towel. "I'm not really sure. I suppose I could travel, and spend all of the money I've earned here, but I think I'll stay here for a while. Mr. Escalle has been coming up with additional responsibilities for me. His business interests are so diversified I readily admit to finding any work I do in this sphere fascinating. I find it refreshing to deal with real world matters rather than ivory tower vagaries. Yes, I believe I will stay on after our Chris departs."

"It's really quite a beautiful place. I can understand why you would. I wish I could find a way to stay." Skylar hoped her fishing wasn't too obvious.

The ease and good humor in his face drained away. "Look, Skylar, you seem like a nice person. I know it's none of my business, but you should leave here, as soon as possible. This isn't the right place for you."

"What do you mean, Cole?"

"I can't explain, but know I'm not speaking frivolously."

"You're the second person to tell me to leave Casa del Mar. What's all the mystery about?"

"Who else told you to go?"

"Luke."

He abruptly stood up and walked over to her. "You have to get out of here. It's imperative. I couldn't bear if someone else…Skylar, you have to leave."

"I'm not going to quit a good job for no reason other than because you and Luke want me to. If there is something specific you're worried about, just tell me."

He gripped the frame of the treadmill and leaned towards her. His blue eyes were anguished and intent, his voice, low. "There was another girl here last summer. Her name was Maia. She disappeared rather mysteriously."

Her heart had begun to pound at the mention of her sister's name. "And? Did you suspect foul play was involved?"

"I don't suspect. I know something terrible happened to her. Maia and I…we were involved. She wasn't the flighty sort. She was studying to be an elementary school teacher. She would never have left without saying anything to me, and I know she would never have run off with another man. That was the official explanation. There was a letter in her handwriting, but someone else must have made her write it."

Skylar decided now was her moment. She stopped the machine, reached out, and covered his hand with her own.

"Cole, I came here because of Maia. She's my sister."

Chapter Twelve

"Maia's sister?" Cole stared at her.

"I came here because of Maia's disappearance. I didn't accept the official explanation either. That's why I applied for the job here."

"How did you get through the interview process? Martin always has potential employees thoroughly vetted."

"My credentials are real, and Maia and I have different last names. We have different fathers. My father died and my mother remarried. There was no reason for Mr. Escalle or anyone else to connect me with Maia. I was even living in a different state, had been for years. It was a gamble, I know, but I had no choice. In her last e-mail to me, Maia wrote she intended to sneak aboard the *Calypso*. Just hours after she sent that e-mail, she disappeared. I think she must have been discovered snooping around the yacht. What do you think?"

"I told her not to go. I begged her. At the time, I didn't know anything about Martin's operation. I had my suspicions, and I kept them to myself, but Maia wouldn't listen to me. She just wouldn't leave it alone. She came to me with what seemed a far-fetched theory about black market weapons. I didn't take her seriously. If only I'd listened to her, maybe…" His voice trailed off in anguished self condemnation.

"Cole, you can't blame yourself. Maia was, no, *is* strong willed. Once she makes up her mind, you can't stop her. I know. But back to that night, she told you she was going to the *Calypso*, too?"

"Yes. I didn't know her plans in advance. I just knew she wanted to get a look on board. She suspected Luke was rendezvousing with other vessels at sea. Once she was gone, I couldn't leave. At first, I stayed because I was hoping she would come back. Now I stay in order to finish what she started. For this reason, I've tried to make myself as useful as possible to Martin. I won't give up until I can nail Luke White."

"Luke?" Surprise and astonishment rang out in her voice.

"Maia's blood is on his hands. He had the *Calypso* out until midmorning on the day she disappeared. He must have been the one who discovered her. I'm going to destroy him. He won't get away with this."

Skylar wondered if it was possible she was completely wrong about Luke. Was she allowing her hormones and her emotions to control her mind? Cole was the second person who was warning her about Luke. "Why do you blame Luke? What about Escalle?"

The entrance door swung wide, and Luke strolled in. In his casual attire of khaki shorts, T-shirt, and sandals, he appeared tan and relaxed, far more beach bum than killer.

"Skylar, I've been looking for you. Lillian told me she saw you come over here. Hello, Cole." There was a curious glint in his eyes as he glanced from her to the other man. The two of them were still leaning very close together, as they had been throughout their conversation.

Now, Skylar straightened up away from Cole, and unconsciously pulled her hand back. "Luke, hi."

She felt vaguely guilty, as if she had been somehow disloyal to Luke by speaking to Cole. She reminded herself she owed him nothing, not yet, and it was up to her to act in Maia's best interests. "This place is quite impressive. I thought I'd get a work out in."

"You didn't swim today?"

"Yes, but I wanted to do some weight training, too."

He glanced obviously at the treadmill.

"I'm just warming up right now," she offered defensively.

Luke stood watching them, making eye contact with one and then the other. Skylar was chagrined to find herself looking down in embarrassment, to avoid meeting his eyes. After a moment, she raised her own defiantly. She wasn't the one who should feel ashamed. He hadn't given her reason to completely trust him.

"How was your work out, Cole?"

"Adequate." Cole's pale eyes were turbulent with emotion. "I was just telling Skylar about Maia. You remember her, don't you, and how she simply vanished one day?"

"Yes, it was strange." Luke didn't hesitate in his response.

"Now Yvette has died. We seem to be having quite a run on bad luck."

"The two situations are hardly similar. Maia took off with some guy, and Yvette OD'd herself."

"Maia didn't run away with another man. That's a lie. She loved me."

"Get real, man. That lady had been brushing you off for some time. Maybe you were the reason she took off. She was a smart girl, clever enough to know that you weren't going to let her go easily. If you're going to get into it, tell Skylar the whole story. All of us knew you and Maia were done, and that she was seeing someone else down in Key West. You were no Romeo to her Juliet."

"You son-of-a-bitch!" Cole lunged straight for Luke, who was ready for him.

Skylar remained frozen, too surprised and too shocked to react. It was all over in a matter of seconds. Despite his size, Luke moved with the fluent grace of a martial arts expert. He somehow caught Cole mid charge, and tossed him over on his back. While Cole was gasping and struggling to breath, Luke flipped him over. The men grappled until Luke managed to draw one of Cole's hands high up on his back, almost up between the shoulder blades. Cole grimaced and continued to squirm, but he was obviously beaten.

"Stop it! Luke, you're hurting him." Skylar hunkered down beside them.

"If I let him up, he's just gonna come after me again. Aren't ya, Cole."

"When I get up, you're fucking dead!" Cole spit into the thick mats, which covered the floor.

"See what I mean," Luke cocked an eyebrow at Skylar. He was barely out of breath. "You're not quite so Ivy League when you're pissed, are you, Cole?"

"Mother F—!" The rest of the expression was lost when Luke pressed his face more firmly down.

"Now we're getting down to the real Cole. All of that education and polish Martin paid for can't hide what you really are."

"Cole, this is stupid," Skylar interrupted.

"I couldn't agree more," Luke muttered. "But you're barking up the wrong tree. I didn't start this. He did, and I don't take kindly to him misleading you about me."

"Why don't you tell her the truth? Tell her where you learned that move you just pulled on me. Tell her you're a fucking assassin. Tell her. Tell her, you son-of-a-bitch. He's Escalle's hired gun. He kills for money. Did you kill Yvette, too, because she was making too much trouble? It couldn't have been too hard. You probably just held a gun to her head and told her to take all of those pills." There was a frantic, nearly hysterical edge to Cole's voice. Granted, he was in pain, but his reaction had a crazed, over-the-top quality to it.

"Shut up, Cole." Luke's tone was serious, deadly serious. "You've said enough."

"Tell her. Tell her, you…Maia…Maia."

Cole's words became progressively more garbled with pain and with, Skylar suspected, sobs.

Luke glanced at her, wordlessly communicating she should step back. He released Cole, being careful to keep his body between Skylar and the other man, but Cole didn't come after him. He appeared completely defeated. Moaning, he pressed his hands to his face, and rocked with his agony.

Luke squatted back down beside him. He patted Cole's shoulder awkwardly. "It's going to be okay, man. Trust me on this one. It's going to be okay."

Cole was lost to all consolation. He rocked on, mutely locked in his pain. Blindly, tears coursing unheeded down his cheeks, he turned to stare out at the sea. "She's out there somewhere, isn't she, Luke?"

"She's out there, Cole, but you two weren't meant to be."

"If there was some way I could be sure that she's alive and okay…"

"If she wanted you to know where she is, she would have contacted you by now."

Luke's words were not sinking in. The other man was too far gone, too emotional, too eaten up with despair.

Luke stood up. He walked over to Skylar and took her hand. He turned to lead her out of the gym.

She hesitated for a moment. "But—"

"He needs some time alone," he said quietly. "He's going to be seriously embarrassed about this anyway, don't make it any worse."

She nodded and allowed him to guide her out into the brilliant sunlight. He didn't hesitate. He walked briskly in the direction of the beach, and didn't say a word to her. The salty, humid sea breeze buffeted her body and tugged at her hair. Once they were on the sand, he grasped her other hand, so that they were standing face to face, with fingers intertwined. His brown eyes were intent upon her.

"You don't know what you're getting into here, Skylar. You're playing with the pros here, and you're strictly amateur. It's noble of you to want to come here and find out what happened to your sister, but it's wrong headed and dangerous. You could end up dead."

"I didn't mean to cause problems between you and Cole."

"Actually, that was probably a good thing. I've known he blames me for Maia's leaving, but he's never spoken with me about it. I knew it was bugging him. He's a sensitive guy, high strung. It was good that he finally let it all out. You can't keep something like that inside, just festering. It'll drive you nuts. Now maybe he'll think about what I said. Your sister was done with him before she took off."

"Wait a minute. How did you find out that Maia is my sister?"

"I did some research on you the morning after you swam out to the *Calypso*. It wasn't difficult."

"Who else knows?"

"I'm not sure. I know Bill has been suspicious of you ever since he found you snooping around the library. He might know. As for Martin, I don't think you would still be here if he'd put it together."

"What's going on, Luke? Bill and Cole both think you were involved with whatever happened to Maia."

"What do you think? Do you trust me?" He released her hands.

Her fingers felt strangely bereft. "I...I don't know what to think."

"That's no answer. You want me to spill my guts to you, but you haven't been straight with me at all. What kind of woman are you, Skylar Connelly? Have you been playing at being *Mata Hari* in order to find out what I know, what I've done? I wonder how far you would have taken your little charade. I probably should have just kept my mouth shut and played along... I have to admit I'm impressed by your loyalty to your sister. By coming here, you put your life on the line. I respect that, but I don't like being manipulated and lied to... I'm an idiot." He shook his head. "I thought maybe there...nothing." He shoved his hands into his pockets.

"What? What are you trying to say? Luke, I wasn't toying with you. I wasn't using you. Well, I was, at first, for Maia's sake, but then, I realized I wanted to be around you for my own sake. It was very confusing for me. I didn't want to like you, but I was attracted to you from the first time I saw you. I didn't become involved with you because of my sister, but in spite of her."

He didn't respond. He stared out at the ocean, refusing to meet her eyes. A muscle at the corner of his jaw twitched. "What's the story now, Skylar? Put your cards on the table."

She swallowed. "All right, I...care about you. That's why it hurts me so much you won't tell me what you know about Maia. Of course, I don't believe you had anything to do with her disappearance. I know you well enough to be confident Cole and Bill are simply wrong."

"Do you?" He stared straight at her. His eyes were cold and distant.

She felt her heart sink. "What do you mean by that?"

"Cole was right about my job. I am sort of a trouble-shooter for Escalle. It's not a nice, clean job. I've gotten my hands dirty more times than I like to remember. Maia was getting into things she had no business in."

"You know what happened to her?"

"Know about it, yeah. I arranged it."

As the horror of his words struck her all she could mumble was, "They were right."

"I've never denied it."

"My God. You killed her."

"No, you little fool. Maia's very much alive."

"Then where is she?"

"I can't tell you. You're just going to have to believe me."

"Why should I believe you? You aren't telling me anything! God, Luke, I want to believe you! You have to know that. But I need something more substantial to go on. Please help me to trust you. I want to tell my mother."

"You can't tell anyone anything right now, especially your mother. Have you spoken to anyone else about your suspicions?"

"After I was shot at, I spoke to the police, but I didn't bring Maia up at all. The officers I spoke with seemed pretty impressed with Escalle. I was considering going to the FBI, but I don't have much hard evidence, just some photographs of guests at the house and some license plate numbers."

"The police are going to steer well clear of this place because they know I'm undercover here. This operation has taken more than a year, and it should be coming to an end in a matter of weeks. Skylar, I'm one of the good guys. I'm very close now, so close I can taste it, but it could all go wrong if either Escalle or Bill suspect anything."

"Are you a cop?"

"No. I'm an ATF agent. You've got to lie low for a little while longer. I promise you Maia is alive and well. You, on the other hand, are in considerable danger. Bill already suspects you, and that means Escalle does, too. I would love it if you could just quit and get out of here. I'm afraid if you did, that might be a red flag to Escalle. I'm so close to nabbing them. If you could stay out of their hair, be invisible, there shouldn't be a problem. Do you understand?"

"Luke, I have so many questions."

"Not now, sweetheart, not now. When this is all over, we'll have all the time in the world." He stepped toward her. She met him. She wrapped her arms around his neck, and pressed ardently up against him. She closed her eyes, and lost herself in the fervent passion of his kiss. His lips were tender, his tongue, caressing, his body lean and firm against her. Her fingers dallied in the moist, silken hair at the nape of his neck.

He was the one who pulled back. "God, you taste incredible. I'd invite you back to my room right now if I didn't have to meet with Bill in half an hour. I don't want to rush our first time together. It may take me days to explore this delicious body of yours."

"A half-an-hour is plenty of time."

He chuckled. The expression in his eyes was hot and hungry. "Don't tempt me. With you around, it's been almost impossible to focus on my job. When you and I finally get together, it's going to be for more than a quickie."

"Quickies can be great stress relievers." She continued to press her body up against his. She felt as if she could melt into him.

"Lady, you make it tough to keep a clear head." He was lowering his lips to hers when she glimpsed a flash of fuchsia out of the corner of her eye. "Luke…Luke. Angelique."

Sure enough, Angelique Whitfield was striding purposefully toward them on the path leading back to the house. She was wearing a stringy, black bathing suit, a fuchsia parreo, and an enormous straw hat with matching fuchsia flowers on its black band. She walked right up to them. Her large, silver-lensed sunglasses effectively hid her eyes and facial expressions.

"Luke, Skylar, how precious. I would never have guessed you went for the outdoorsy type." This last bit was addressed to Luke. "I thought your taste was more, oh, how shall I put it, sophisticated."

"I've always liked athletic women." The look he sent Skylar fairly smoldered.

"A pity, but one can't argue taste. Nevertheless, Luke, I do need to speak with you privately." She removed her sunglasses. Her eyes appeared brilliantly blue against the ocean backdrop.

Skylar was impressed with the quality of her colored contact lenses.

"All right, Angelique. Skylar, are you free tomorrow afternoon?"

"Yeah. I guess. I don't think I have anything going on."

"Meet me at the dock around two. Stay out of trouble." He caressed her cheek with his fingertips, offered her a wink, and then walked away with the other woman.

Skylar was left wondering what had just happened. The man certainly did run hot and cold. But if he was an agent on an investigation… It was this 'but' that made her cringe hours later. She desperately wanted to believe him, but what proof did she have he was who he said he was? How could she be sure Maia was even alive? All he'd given her was his word. This equivocating was driving her crazy. She decided she would no longer go back and forth on the issue of trusting Luke. She was ready to make a leap of faith.

Chapter Thirteen

Later that same day, Skylar glared balefully at her laptop screen. As she had nothing else of critical importance to accomplish, she was blowing time actually working on her thesis. Suddenly, the phone in her bedroom rang. She picked up the receiver. "Hello?"

"Skylar, it's Lillian. Forgive me for interrupting your private time, but Mr. Escalle has asked me to invite you to an informal dinner this evening. He is sorry for the short notice. I told him a young woman like you probably already had plans for a Friday night, but he insisted." She sounded disapproving.

Abstractly, Skylar wondered what other plans Lillian might think she had. After all, she had only been out once during her entire time at Casa del Mar. Lillian could hardly have pegged her as a party animal. "I have no plans for tonight. Dinner sounds great. When you say dinner is informal, does that entail a dress?"

"Not necessarily, just dress comfortably. You're going out on the *Calypso*, and the ocean breezes can be quite chilling at night. Please be at the dock around seven o'clock."

"Thanks, Lillian. I'll look forward to it."

"It should be a very pleasant evening." There was a strange edge to Lillian's voice that belied her closing statement. Skylar was left to ponder this, as well as why her boss would go to the effort of including a relatively insignificant employee for an evening aboard his yacht. There was only one surefire way to find out the answer to both of these questions. She went over to her closet to consider possible outfits.

When Skylar meandered down to the *Calypso*, the extraordinary sunset was not yet complete. They were an aspect of life at Casa del Mar she would genuinely regret leaving behind. They were brilliant with all of the color, passion, and power that characterized a tropical paradise. Aboard the docked yacht, several crewmembers were still scurrying about like ants on an anthill. To her surprise, Martin Escalle, who was standing by the gangplank, greeted her.

"Skylar, welcome aboard." He held out a hand, but made no effort to step down to her. For the few brief seconds it took her to cross into the yacht, he was taller than she. He had to look up to her when she stood before him. She was perversely glad she had chosen to wear her very high-heeled, cork sandals.

Instead of his usual dark suit, Escalle's neat figure was nattily attired in oatmeal linen pants and a bold, peacock blue, silk shirt. His casually elegant appearance was completed with expensive, tasseled, cordovan, Italian loafers. His opened collar revealed a heavy gold medallion on a thick chain around his neck. His apparel showcased his George Hamilton-esque tan.

"You look lovely tonight, completely charming," he congratulated her with a smile exposing his almost too white, perfect teeth. He clearly approved of her embroidered peasant blouse and purple, jewel-cuffed capris.

She became uncomfortably aware of how his eyes lingered on her breasts. For such a mature and sophisticated man, he was displaying a remarkable lack of couth and a disturbing degree of interest in her. She decided she would do best to appear oblivious to both. "Thank you, and thank you also for including me this evening. To be honest, I've been dying to go out on the *Calypso*."

"She's one of the completely perfect joys of my life. I do like to share her with those who can appreciate her." Taking her hand, he wrapped her arm around his own. She caught a waft of a heady and rich cologne. "I'm aware you are a true daughter of Poseidon. So, I feel I have been remiss in not taking you out before now." He led her inside to a large, exquisite lounge decorated in shades that called to mind a conch shell, peach, cream, beige, and some daring hints of salmon. The room was trimmed in blond wood, and an elaborate, pink marble bar with a mirrored backdrop dominated one side. The overall effect was one of expensive and decadent comfort.

Angelique was already seated there. She had a glass of wine in her hand. "Skylar," she said, nodding a cool greeting.

"Hello, Mrs. Whitfield."

"Please make yourself comfortable, Skylar," Escalle directed. "Angelique and I have been enjoying a very fine Chablis Premier Cru. Would you care for a glass?"

"That sounds good." Skylar sat down adjacent to Angelique.

"I know my sister has been concerned about your work with Christopher, but I made her watch the two of you today. She agrees your progress has been astounding, miraculous even. We both owe you our thanks."

He handed her a long-stemmed, delicate wine glass filled with a pale golden wine. She took a tasting sip, and found it fresh, light, and fruity without being overly sweet. "This is really nice."

"I am glad you like it."

"Skylar," Angelique spoke up. "I've lacked faith in your abilities. I see now I was wrong. I was being an overprotective mother. Chris has really progressed in overcoming his fear of the water under your tutelage. Thank you." The expression in those dark eyes was disarmingly direct. There was no sign of the sarcastic, self-absorbed woman whom Skylar had encountered earlier that day on the beach.

"Chris is a great kid. It's been fun working with him. He's actually quite a decent athlete. He's certainly competitive enough."

"That quality definitely comes from our side of the family," Escalle quipped, as he patted his sister's knee. "It's so good to hear that. I was worried the boy was rather…weak, like his father."

"Jim wasn't weak. He was a gentle spirit. You just didn't relate well with him," Angelique said.

This was the first time Skylar ever heard Angelique disagree with her brother.

"How could I, when he would have nothing to do with me, or allow you to, for that matter? Come now, let's not air this tired, old argument in front of Skylar. Let's return to the subject of Christopher. Do you feel he will be ready for St. Mark's in the fall?"

"Of course, I can't speak of Chris' academic progress, but in terms of athletics and socialization, he should do just fine. He and Tyler, Conny's nephew, are good friends. Chris takes instruction well. He's a good listener. I have no real concerns, but I'm not familiar with the school. Could you tell me something about it?"

"St. Mark's is the most exclusive all boys prep school in Palm Beach," Escalle offered.

"I'm not sure he's ready for a boarding school yet, Martin. He's so young."

"Angelique, we've been through this. It's a fabulous school. I wish I had had the opportunity to attend a school like St. Mark's. The facilities are incredible, and you've seen the list of the colleges the graduates attend. All of those boys go on to Ivy League institutions. He'll be able to come home for weekends and vacations. It's an ideal situation all around."

"I know. It's just that he's my baby."

"My sister's maternal instinct is rather overly developed."

"What do you think, Skylar? Is he ready for boarding school?"

Skylar shifted in her seat. This was not the sort of question she wanted to field. "It sounds like a great school, but if you don't like the idea of Chris boarding, aren't there any worthwhile day schools near your home in Miami?"

"Well, actually," Angelique began, but then her brother interrupted.

"St. Mark's is the right school for the boy. It offers rigorous academic and athletic programs, and the boarding aspect will provide the boy with a consistent and disciplined environment. You know you are often away and very busy with all of your charitable activities. It will be better for both of you for Chris to simply live there. After a few months, when you see how smoothly it all goes, you will be praising my foresight."

Skylar felt sorry for Chris. It sounded like his uncle was really eager to make sure he was out of the picture. It seemed to her Escalle was actively trying to drive a wedge between Angelique and her son. It was puzzling; on the one hand, he provided abundantly for the boy, but then he didn't want him around.

Much as she liked Chris and worried about him, she had more pressing concerns at the moment. She still had absolutely no idea why she had been invited aboard the *Calypso*.

Suddenly, there was the soft purr of a powerful engine started.

"We're underway. If you will excuse me, ladies, I want to have a word with Luke."

Escalle's departure left Skylar sitting alone with Angelique. The silence was awkward.

"It's really a beautiful boat." Skylar offered, glancing around.

"Yes, it is." Angelique responded automatically. "It's Martin's pride and joy."

"It's quite large, isn't it?"

"You'll have to ask Martin for the exact specifications. There are four staterooms, this lounge, a dining room, and a galley kitchen. It's all very comfortable, but I only go out on her for my brother's sake. I hate this boat."

"You hate it?" How could one hate complete luxury and ease when combined with the power and majesty of the ocean?

"Yes. I wish Martin would sell it, but he never will. The *Calypso* is his only real hobby. My husband, Jim, drowned after he fell from the deck of this yacht. Chris witnessed his father's death. That's why he's so terrified of the ocean."

"Oh, I'm sorry. I didn't mean to be intrusive."

"It's all right. It was a horrible accident. Jim had had too much to drink. He and Martin never got along. In fact, Martin didn't approve of my marrying Jim. We didn't see my brother much until Chris was about five. Martin invited us down here to celebrate Chris' birthday, and to sort of reconcile our differences. We all went out on this boat, and then Jim died. There's nothing more to it." As Angelique told her story, she stared at the sea, which appeared nearly purple in the dimming light. Her expression was distant, focused on the tragic past rather than on Skylar and the present.

"That's a horrible memory for a child."

"Yes. He's coped with it very well, I believe, and the therapists I've taken Chris to have concurred." She carefully slid her index finger under each of her eyes to remove all traces of tears before the moisture could cause her mascara to run. "His absolute phobia of the water has been the only obvious lingering problem. I have to admit, you've helped him work through his fear more effectively than any of those therapists."

"He's not completely over it. He'll swim in the pool, but I haven't yet been able to get him near the ocean."

"He is actually swimming in the pool. Before you came, the only water he would get into was his bathtub. Today, I saw him laughing and splashing in the pool just like any other kid. I can't describe how that made me feel."

"All is well," Escalle announced as he rejoined them. "As usual, Luke has matters well in hand. We will dine once he has located a satisfactory spot. Skylar, I like to be far enough out so all that I can see of the land is the glittering of very distant lights. There is something so pleasurable, so romantic about dining out on the water." He sauntered directly to the bar where the wine bottle was chilling in a crystal ice bucket. He brought the bottle over to the ladies and topped off their glasses. Then, he finished off the bottle in his own glass. He swirled his glass in an elegant fashion, and then took a sip.

For a while, the three of them enjoyed their wine and chatted about mundane matters. Skylar found both of her companions bright and witty. They applied themselves to entertaining her. To her surprise, she was enjoying herself.

Then, Escalle abruptly shifted gears. "Skylar, as we have expressed already, we are very happy with your work, but have decided that it would be best for Chris to start to participate in activities with other boys. Don't you agree?"

"Oh yes. Completely. He has thrived on the camaraderie and competition he has shared with Tyler. He's very ready for more interaction with kids his own age."

"We're so glad you agree. Of course, we will all be sorry to see you go. You have been a very pleasant addition to our little circle."

Skylar swallowed hard. She hadn't anticipated this turn of events at all. What had precipitated it?

"When would you like me to leave?"

"Please don't be offended." He offered her a sympathetic glance.

"It's in part because you have done such a fine job that Chris is now ready to move on," Angelique said. "I'm sorry I haven't been more supportive, but it would be best for Chris to be with other boys."

"He has genuinely enjoyed his time with Tyler," Skylar reiterated, completely at a loss as to what to say and how to proceed.

"We would like you to stay on through the end of the month. Of course, you will be paid for the remaining time we had contracted with you," Escalle concluded.

"If you want to stay in the Keys for a while, I'm sure Lillian or Conny could you help you find reasonable accommodations."

Three weeks! It wasn't very much time at all. Could she figure out what had really happened to Maia before her time ran out? Despite her anxiety, she forced herself to present a calm, relaxed façade. "It's very generous of you to offer, but I can't accept payment from you if I don't earn it."

"Nonsense. Of course you can. Besides, we did have an agreement, and I am responsible for changing the term of employment. You are entitled to those wages, as I am sure any attorney versed in labor law will agree. I will also throw in a bonus for a job well done. The extra time should help you complete your thesis. How is it coming?"

"It's coming along slowly but surely. Well, thank you. I'll be sorry to leave your beautiful house. I've really enjoyed my time here." Skylar smiled and sipped her wine. Escalle was very eager to get rid of her. He was paying her off to facilitate her departure. She decided he must be suspicious of her.

The rest of the evening passed painfully slowly for her. She was on edge the entire time, and very attentive to both the mood and the conversation. Though she desperately wanted to be off the boat, she chatted and smiled through the exquisite meal. Afterwards, while having coffee, she *oohed* and *aahed* over the panorama of stars. She longed for a glimpse of Luke, but he stayed out of sight in the pilothouse. She was greatly relieved when the *Calypso* finally returned to the dock.

Escalle escorted her ashore while Angelique remained aboard.

"Thank you for a lovely dinner." Skylar said, eager to return to the sanctuary of her bedroom.

"It was a pleasant evening. I enjoyed your company." Then, taking her wholly by surprise, he reached out and took her hand. He raised it to his lips. "You are so confident and strong, and yet so lovely. I find these qualities admirable in a woman." He stared intently at her face, as if studying it. "I may be making a mistake letting you go. Perhaps you would consider staying on here under different circumstances, without the responsibility of a small boy?"

Chapter Fourteen

Completely unsure of where this was heading, she responded. "What sort of job do you have in mind?"

For such a slender man, his chuckle came from surprisingly deep in his chest. "Skylar, I am not offering you employment. Tell me, did you enjoy your evening?"

"Yes, very much."

"As did I, and I had not anticipated the pleasure I derived from your company. When I decide I want something, I act immediately. I'm a very wealthy and generous man. I think you are wasted as a swimming coach for my nephew."

"I really enjoy teaching him and playing with him."

"How would you feel about 'playing' with me?"

"But…But you barely know me."

"I know more about you than I imagine most of your former lovers have. Have you provided them with resumés and references? There is the small matter of a physical exam, and some blood work. I believe in entering into such arrangements with all cards on the table. Don't you agree? The agreement is quite simple, but mutually satisfying. I will support you in the lap of luxury for as long as we suit, then we can amicably go our separate ways, with you a much wealthier woman."

"I…um have to think about it." Wanting to end the conversation, she took a step back away from him though he still held her hand. She didn't want to be packing her bags that same night. However, she had no idea of how to handle this development. Diplomacy was definitely the order of the day.

"Excuse me, Mr. Escalle." Luke's deep, familiar tones broke in, causing Escalle to release her hand.

"Yes, Luke?"

"I don't mean to interrupt, but I'd like to speak with you as soon as possible."

"Is there a problem?"

Luke glanced at Skylar. His expression was cold and remote. "I would prefer to discuss this matter privately."

"Of course. Ms. Connelly, please consider my offer. Good night." Her dapper employer followed Luke back to the *Calypso*.

Dazedly, she made her way back to her room. She didn't know what to make of the entire evening. Luke appeared genuinely angry with her. His eyes had been brutally unsympathetic when they had encountered hers. Had he overheard any of her conversation with Escalle? Could he believe she was interested in her employer? The man was old enough to be her father, and was most likely a criminal.

If Luke could believe something like that about her, then he couldn't think very highly of her.

Then there was the issue of Escalle, himself. She had, in no way, anticipated this development. She wondered how much time he was going to give her to consider her answer. Was she still supposed to leave after the designated three weeks? Or was this all a game to confuse her because Escalle and Stevens suspected her?

Skylar had so much on her mind, so many different worries to consider, she couldn't sleep. Reading a book proved futile as she found herself rereading the same line again and again. She turned on the radio, but found the music irritating, not soothing. To make matters worse, her stomach was growling because she had barely touched her dinner. It was nearly one when she threw back her covers. Despite the late hour, she decided to go down to the kitchen and rummage around for a snack.

As she headed down the hall, she found the mansion very still and silent. No lights were on, but the moon was very bright, and as there were large windows everywhere, she had no problem finding her way down to the gourmet kitchen where Rene ruled. She flipped on one of the light switches. She had only been in the room a handful of times, generally to procure afternoon snacks for Chris. Rene didn't appreciate intruders in his immaculately clean domain. Still, she knew in which cabinet she would find the glasses, as well as where the crackers and cookies were stored. The massive pair of silver Sub Zero refrigerators were fully stocked, and she quickly found the milk.

All of a sudden, brilliant, white light flooded the kitchen. In reaction, she dropped the carton of milk.

"Oh, my dear," Lillian fluttered. "I scared you! I'm sorry." She was in a mint green, terrycloth robe and bedroom slippers. Her hair was up in rollers and covered with a scarf.

"I was just getting a snack." Skylar knelt to pick up the half-empty carton. She glanced around desperately at all of the uncluttered, gleaming silver and black granite surfaces. "Do you have any idea where Rene keeps the paper towels?"

"Right over here." Lillian disappeared into the closet-like cupboard and emerged with a roll of paper towels. She started to wipe up the spilled milk.

"Lillian, please, let me."

"Don't you worry. I've…Oops." The two women bumped heads.

"Clumsy me," Lillian chuckled.

"Me, too. I'll get this mess." In short order, Skylar finished cleaning it up.

"As good as new," Lillian offered from where she sat perched on a stool. In the bright light, without any makeup, she looked surprisingly young and pretty.

"Lillian, you have really lovely skin."

"Thank you. I'm quite vain about it. My mother always told me a woman's skin should feel like a magnolia petal. What are you doing up so late?"

"I couldn't get to sleep."

"When I was your age, I had no problem sleeping. Now, I find that I have to read sometimes, or I do needlepoint. Both relax me, but you shouldn't have any trouble sleeping. You're so active, too. Is something bothering you, my dear?"

"I do have some things on my mind."

"Would you like to talk about them? I'm a good listener."

"You sound just like my mother."

"I would be so proud to have a daughter like you. It's one of the disappointments of my life that I never had children of my own."

"But you're part of the Escalle family, and you and Chris seem to have a good relationship."

Lillian smiled as she rose to her feet. She bustled over to the refrigerator, opened the door, and peered in. "They are all special to me, and that boy is such a blessing. Now, let's see. I know Rene has some delicious cheeses here somewhere. At lunchtime, there was a Brie that absolutely made my mouth water. Here's some crusty French bread. Do you like red grapes? They're seedless."

"Everything sounds delicious."

In short order, Lillian pulled together a tasty snack. They had cheese on warmed French bread with grapes and milk. They chatted easily. Lillian expressed interest in Skylar's future plans, and Skylar had the older woman laughing at vignettes from her coaching experiences. All in all, it was a very pleasant time.

"I will miss you, my dear. I have so enjoyed your company."

"To be honest, the news I'm no longer needed here came as a complete surprise to me."

Lillian nodded sympathetically.

"My contract was for two more months. I was to have finished up at the end of May. Of course, Mr. Escalle has offered to pay me for the full time. That was very generous of him."

"Yes, Martin is a giving man."

"Why do you think…I mean, what do you think changed? Both Ms. Whitfield and Mr. Escalle said they thought I'd done a good job with Chris. Though he is much less phobic of water, Chris is by no means a proficient swimmer yet. I'm just surprised they don't want me to finish the job. Were they dissatisfied with me for some other reason?"

"Truthfully, I have no idea. Angelique can be difficult when it comes to Chris. Maybe it was simply a matter of his mother being jealous of your good relationship with the boy."

Skylar nodded politely, though it was obvious to her that Lillian was dissembling. Angelique was not the decision maker at Casa del Mar, even with respect to her own son.

"Skylar, I wanted to ask you… You must forgive me if I'm being intrusive, but I'm curious." She leaned forward conspiratorially. "You are leaving Casa del Mar, aren't you?"

"Yes, eventually. I'm not sure."

"I'll be frank with you, my dear. After your outing on the *Calypso*, Martin and I spoke. He mentioned he wanted me to redecorate the suite that adjoins his own. At first, I thought he wanted it changed because that poor girl was found dead in there, but then he said I should speak with you. I don't mean to be nosey. It's only that I thought you and Luke had an understanding. Now, I'm confused. I'm going to ask you this directly. Are you and Martin involved?"

Skylar repressed a shudder at the thought of moving into a bedroom, albeit a redecorated one, where another woman had recently died. "Mr. Escalle asked me if I was interested in a more…intimate relationship. I haven't given him my answer yet."

"Ah," She nodded sagely. "I do understand. I had hoped…Martin remains a very virile man, and an overwhelmingly attractive one. He has a fascination with much younger women. I find it peculiar. One would think that a man of his intellect and abilities could see beyond a pretty face and a youthful body. I don't mean to disparage you, Skylar, but a creature like Yvette? I know it's very inappropriate to speak ill of the deceased, but what could he have had in common with that trollop?" Lillian's tone was calm enough, but her expression was both disappointed and angry.

"Yvette was very beautiful."

"Yes, but one does have to get out of the bed sometime, and she was a complete failure as a hostess for Martin. Her manners were appalling, and there wasn't a thought in her head. Over the years, I've watched an endless parade of Yvettes. Not one of them was a suitable life partner for Martin. That is my one consolation, you know. They come and go, and I always stay right by his side."

"I know he appreciates you, Lillian. He speaks of you with the highest regard and respect," Skylar observed, well aware this was not what Lillian wanted to hear.

"Yes. I know." Her expression was disgruntled in the extreme. She shook her head, and then patted the back of her hair. Just as quickly, the irritation was gone from her countenance. She now wore her usual serene mask. "Do you realize we've been chatting for almost an hour? If I don't get to bed soon I won't be good for anything tomorrow."

"I'll clean up, and then I'll head up, too. Thank you for talking with me. I feel more relaxed now."

"It's been my pleasure. Since Martin has always moved around so much, it's proven difficult for me to make real friends over the years. Good night now."

"Sleep well, Lillian."

"Goodness, let's hope that I can make up for quantity with quality." She paused half way to the kitchen door. "Do let me know what you decide with respect to Yvette's bedroom."

Skylar nodded acquiescence. She was desperate to find out what had happened to Maia, but moving into Yvette's bedroom was definitely not the way she intended to go about it. Luke was going to come through for her, she had to have faith. But she wasn't going to reveal her hand to Lillian. She didn't want Escalle, through his housekeeper, to know what her plans were, at least not for a few more days.

* * * *

"Good job, Chris. Your kick is really getting stronger. We should try some backstrokes."

"Aw, come on, Skylar, let's play a game," Tyler whined.

"In a few minutes, Tyler. Let's get the work part done with first."

"Then we can play water polo?" Chris asked.

"All right." She chuckled. "If you two do a good job." She had come up with a modified version of the water sport that both boys enjoyed immensely. It was more like 'monkey in the middle' than actual water polo, but it did get Chris swimming around and not thinking about his fears. Over time, the game had progressed from the shallow end to the deeper water.

When they finished in the pool, she followed the boys over to the men's locker room. "Hurry up. We're running late. Tyler, your Dad is going to be here to pick you up right after lunch. So, no goofing off. Just get showered and changed. We're supposed to have lunch at twelve thirty."

"Sure, Skylar."

"No problemo." Tyler smirked before letting go of the door, so that it slammed shut in her face.

The kid really was a devil. Still, he was good for Chris, who needed a little spunk. Wiping her face off on her towel, she stepped into the ladies' changing room The two locker rooms were right next to each other, and the walls weren't particularly thick, so she could hear a lot of what was going on next door. She smiled to herself. Those two little monkeys sounded like they were having a blast. They had been full of beans all morning.

Suddenly, she was gripped by the forearm, spun about, and pushed up against the wall. The salmon colored tile was cool against her skin, but not as cold as the expression in Luke's brown eyes. He grabbed her other arm, pinning her. But, despite his apparent fury, he held her there loosely. She knew she could easily pull away from him.

"I don't know how long you've playing both sides of the field, Skylar, but let me make myself clear, don't interfere, or I will take you out of the game."

He hadn't raised his voice, but she was frightened. This ruthless, threatening stranger had nothing in common with her laid back Luke.

"Luke, you don't understand."

"I understand very well actually. Lillian informed me you aren't leaving here after all. You are going to stay on as Escalle's new piece of ass. Do you have any idea how much of a hassle it was to convince him to fire you? I wanted you to be safe," he hissed. "All of that crap about your sister, you really had me going. That and those sweet, haunted eyes of yours…It's all been about money for you, hasn't it?"

"You're wrong, Luke. I came here to find out about Maia."

"All right. I'll give you that. Then you got down here and figured Escalle was the ticket to easy street. It doesn't matter now anyway. You played me for a fool. I'm not the first guy that it's happened to, but don't get in my way when it comes to Escalle. If you even think of blowing my cover, know that I'll make sure you never see Maia again."

"Luke, you're completely wrong here. I have no intention of becoming involved with Escalle. I never have. I can't stand the man." Skylar was shocked at his ruthlessness.

He appeared momentarily nonplussed. "That's not what Lillian said," he blustered. "I've found that when something stinks, it's generally rotten."

"Luke…" She tugged her wrists free of his hold, and placed her hands on his chest. "The man is creepy, a criminal, a good fifteen years older than I am, and his last girlfriend died rather suspiciously and conveniently for him. Those aren't even the main reasons I wouldn't have anything to do with him." She took a deep breath. "I'm involved with you."

"I don't think I can afford your tab."

Something he had said had just registered in her mind. "You got me fired? Why? I wasn't getting in the way of your investigation."

"I was an idiot. I wanted to keep you safe, out of the line of fire. It wasn't easy actually. I had to convince him you were up to no good, but that you were no threat to him or to the operation. It took some work, but I got the job done." He bit out sarcastically. "Stay out of my way." In disgust, he turned away, and strode out the door.

For a moment, she stood staring at the swinging door. Then, she took off after him. "Luke! Luke, wait! Listen to me." She was in the corridor chasing after him when Chris popped out of the men's locker room.

"Hey, Skylar, could you turn on the hot tub jets for us?"

She watched Luke disappear out into the bright sunlight. She exhaled slowly. She couldn't go after him now, but she intended to later. She had to make him believe her.

"*Pl-eeease*, Skylar." The boy looked up at her with a winsomely hopeful expression, the absence of several teeth added to his overall charm.

"No, Chris. You know you're not allowed in the hot tub. It's for grown ups."

"My mom lets me get into the hot tub with her."

"That's her prerogative. She's your mother. I'm not."

"Aw, come on."

"The answer is no, and will remain no. No matter how many times you ask me. Now, please go and get changed."

"What'd Luke want?"

"Just to check up on us."

"Luke is so cool."

"Chris," she admonished. "Come on. Hurry up."

"We'll be ready in a second. Tyler, she said 'no'."

The shouted words carried back to her as the door swung shut.

That afternoon, Skylar looked for any opportunity to speak with Luke, but he was either too busy or avoiding her. She felt growing pressure. Escalle was awaiting her answer. She was greatly relieved when she learned he had left for Miami to attend to some business matters.

She needed to talk with Luke, and desperation drove her to act.

She'd observed whenever Escalle was out of town, Luke took the *Calypso* out at night. There were two ways to interpret this behavior, either, Escalle wanted to be out of town during the delivery of his contraband goods, for that's what she suspected was taking place, or his lieutenant was the criminal.

She had long since dismissed the second possibility. Luke was a good man. She was sure of it. Still, she guessed the *Calypso* would be going out that night. With sudden clarity and determination, she decided she would be aboard the sleek yacht the next time it left dock. By doing so, she guessed she would find the answers to many of her questions. She was aware Maia disappeared following a similar expedition, but Skylar wouldn't let this sway her. In fact, it spurred her on.

Unlike Maia, however, she decided to leave a trail. She sat down at her laptop to e-mail Laura. To her immense dismay, she found that her server was down. She wasn't comfortable using the telephone at Casa Del Mar to call her friend. She even considered calling her mother. However, she realized telling Anna Brendan anything would result in her mother immediately calling the police.

Finally, she sat down and wrote a note. Then, she proceeded down the hall, to Cole's bedroom. She knocked, and waited a moment. There was no answer. She opened the door and went it. She glanced around the tidy room, debating where she should leave her note. She wanted to put it in a safe place, but one where he was sure to discover it. There was a thick, hardback book on the table by the bed. She crossed over to it, and picked it up. It was entitled "*John Smith.*" One page about half way through was dog-eared down? She slipped the folded envelope inside the book at that place. She guessed Cole was one of those people who read in order to fall asleep. She hoped he would find her note that very night.

In it, she asked him to help her, for Maia's sake. She explained she intended to sneak aboard the *Calypso* that night, and she asked him to contact the authorities and her friend Laura Samuels if she didn't return within twenty-four hours.

She debated letting Cole know about the safety deposit box, but decided against it. It sufficed Laura knew about it. Skylar hoped she'd compiled enough evidence to get the police to take a serious look at the goings on at Casa del Mar, just in case.

After leaving the note, she hurried out of the house and down to her car. Miracle of miracles, it started. Gripping the steering wheel, Skylar silently thanked Luke for fixing it. At the thought of him, she bit at her thumbnail, overwhelmed by feelings of danger and uncertainty. He was convinced she'd played him for a fool, and she'd not yet had the opportunity to correct his impression. She seriously doubted by sneaking aboard the yacht he captained she would enhance his opinion of her.

She drove to a nearby bait shop/convenience store, a run down, ramshackle building that looked like any serious wind would knock it down.

She wandered through the crowded aisles. Moe's was stocked with odds and ends and bits of everything, from shell earrings and necklaces, to dishwashing soap, ravioli, beach towels, and some hardware.

"You need any help?" The clerk called out to her. A white-haired, skin-tanned-to-the-color-of-bacon conch, was sitting behind the register reading a newspaper with a cigar clamped between his large, yellow stained teeth.

"No, I'm fine. Thanks." She picked out a couple of granola bars, a bottle of water, and one of soda, and a small flashlight. She carried her acquisitions up to the register.

"Let's see what we have here." The clerk set his cigar down, and began to type on his ancient cash register.

Skylar barely managed to control her impatience. She wanted to get aboard the *Calypso* and locate a decent hiding place before Luke and his crew started preparing her for the night run.

"Is that all?"

"Yes, that's it." As she held out a twenty, she glimpsed a long, wickedly curved diving knife in the display case on top of which the cash register sat. "No, I want this knife, too."

"This one's a honey. You know how to handle a knife like this?"

"Yes." She didn't want to continue the discussion.

"Anything else?"

"No, that's it." She glanced at her watch. It read three-fifteen. That didn't leave her much time. "I don't mean to be rude, but I'm in something of a hurry, so if you don't mind," she gestured at her purchases.

"All right, lady. No need to get testy." He put her goods into a brown paper bag, which she immediately tucked into her backpack.

"Do you have a ladies' room around here?"

"Sure. Here's the key. It's right around the back."

The bathroom was surprisingly clean. Skylar flipped the toilet closed with her tennis shoe and put her bag on top of it. She pulled out a pair of lightweight, dark blue sweat pants, a black t-shirt, dark socks, and a sports bra. She changed hurriedly, and then worked her hair into a French braid. She peered into the mirror over the sink. She decided she didn't look that suspicious. Her clothing was dark, but was clearly athletic wear, something one would wear while jogging.

Now came the scary part of the whole deal. She drove Bessy down to a public section of beach. She parked her there. She told Lillian she was going out. Her story wouldn't be convincing if her car remained at the house.

She pulled on her backpack, and tightened it on her shoulders. Then, she went out on the beach. Skylar began to jog just along that line where the waves washed and then receded. She easily dodged the water, and found the sand firm and easy to run on. She soon crossed onto private property. She guessed most of the owners wouldn't mind because she was staying close to the water's edge, a practice she'd seen many joggers employ. The fences and gates that separated properties generally ended before the sand.

It was a good mile and a half to Casa del Mar, so she was starting to sweat by the time the stucco walls came into view. She jogged her way down to the dock. Skylar kept her eyes opened, watching for anybody or any activity. The *Calypso* was silently resting at the dock. As she slowed to a walk, she could hear the water lapping gently on the yacht's sides. Skylar strolled casually toward the boat, hoping to appear as if she was just admiring the vessel.

She put her foot on the gangplank. Still, all remained silent and calm, and there was no one in sight. She stepped up. It was now or never.

Refusing to take another glance over her shoulder, she walked onboard. With a sweating palm, she reached for the door handle leading into the main salon where she'd met with Escalle and his sister. To her immense relief, it turned easily in her hand.

All of the lights were off inside, and the Roman shades blocked most of the golden afternoon sun. She passed through exquisite double doors into the formal dining room, and then into a fully equipped galley kitchen. She returned to the dining room, and took the other door. She tiptoed her way into a short corridor. Her heart was in her throat.

She opened the first door she encountered, and stared into a luxurious stateroom. Another door led into another, slightly smaller boudoir. She shut this door, too. Neither room seemed to offer good hiding places. At the end of the corridor, she descended a spiral staircase. A metal door with a porthole led into a snack bar area with a laundry room tucked into the back of it. Thankfully, this room was also empty and still, and eerily dark without the large windows of the rooms on the level above. Next, there was a tidy bunkroom as well as a much smaller, more utilitarian stateroom.

A final door led to the yacht's innards. She was in some sort of machine room. Though it was very dark in the bowels of the *Calypso*, she proceeded on. She moved with her hands extended out before her, feeling her way. Then, she bumped her toe on something hollow and metallic. The sound rang out. She cringed in fear, and held her breath, but nothing happened in reaction. She remained alone. She wondered how long she had been aboard. It seemed as if she had been wandering around the massive yacht for a long time. She was aware she had to hurry, someone was bound come on the ship soon. She had to have a hiding place before that happened.

She took her backpack off. She felt around inside until she found her flashlight. She turned it on. The beam was bright but narrow. She ducked under some large pipes and found herself facing yet another door. This one was substantial and locked. Through the glass porthole, she beamed her flashlight into the room, but could only make out some dark, square shapes. She tried the knob again. No luck.

Immensely frustrated, she peered in again. Could these boxes contain Escalle's contraband materials? She was so close it was maddening. If this one door had been unlocked, like all of the others on board, she would probably have a pretty good idea of how Martin Escalle made his living, and of why her sister disappeared. She wondered if these guns or drugs or whatever was the reason the *Calypso* went out after dusk almost every night.

But then again, this scenario was too simplistic, she realized. This room was in no way hidden. Escalle and his men were confident and successful, not careless. Escalle would never be so foolish as to store his illegal goods in an obvious place aboard his own vessel. It was then that an answer dawned on her; the important thing was not what was on the *Calypso*, but who. She guessed Escalle used the yacht as a meeting place that was outside of the scrutiny of Customs or Immigration authorities. He could meet with drug kingpins or terrorists out on international waters, and thereby avoid tarnishing his reputation.

Luke was clearly privy to many of those meetings. She had to believe he was who he said he was, an ATF agent who was close to nabbing Escalle. By sneaking aboard the *Calypso*, she had placed her life in his hands.

Suddenly, she heard a door slam.

Chapter Fifteen

Skylar jumped at the noise. Her heart racing, she flipped off the flashlight, and ran lightly back through the engine room. It didn't seem a good hiding place. If the *Calypso* was heading out to sea, it was likely for this room soon to be occupied. Her braid caught on something. She jerked it free. Back out in the corridor, she stared at the silver door leading into the galley. She could hear footsteps above her, and the distant timbre of masculine voices.

Shit! She had to hide. But where? Even though the *Calypso* was a large yacht, Luke often took her out alone or with minimal assistance, she reasoned. So, it was unlikely anyone would be sleeping in the bunkroom on this night. She opened the door to the bunkroom, and stepped inside. To her dismay, there was nowhere to hide, just two sets of bunk beds on either side of the narrow room.

There was another constricted door opposite her. She hurried over to it, opened it, and found herself in a very tight bathroom. A toilet, narrow shower stall, and a sink were jammed into the tiny space. She stepped into the stall, and pulled the shower curtain closed behind her. She struggled to breathe quietly, though her lungs were begging for air because of her sprint and her nerves. She wished she had had more time to find a hiding place, but this bathroom was the best she could do under the circumstances.

She heard footsteps and then voices. There was definitely more than one man out there. She slid down the wall until she was seated with her knees tight against her chest. She knew she was being goofy, but she wanted to be as small as physically possible. The voices became more distant as their possessors must have gone into the engine room. Then, she heard heavy footsteps going back up the steps. Realizing she was likely to remain in the bathroom for some time, she shifted in an attempt to get more comfortable.

Time passed agonizingly slowly. Her watch had a light on it, so she was aware less than an hour had passed. She had no intention of moving from her hiding place until the *Calypso* was at sea, so Luke couldn't simply escort her back ashore.

A humming from the *Calypso's* engines woke her. Despite the yacht's very sophisticated ride stabilizers, because of her location in the bowels of the ship, Skylar had an awareness of movement. She was amazed she managed to doze off, considering how nervous she had been. She glanced down at her watch, and hit the little light. It was seven-fifteen.

Her stomach growled. The noise was startling in the dark quiet of her shower stall. She realized she was hungry. She unzipped her backpack, rooted around, pulled out a granola bar, opened it up, and munched slowly. She sipped at her bottled water. Under the circumstances, she was reasonably comfortable, she reassured herself.

Her long legs were cramped, but there was no way she could stretch them out. She wondered where the *Calypso* was going, whether Luke was steering her, and whether Cole had gotten her note yet.

Wondering about Cole got her thinking about Maia. She reached up to touch her dolphin pendant, as she often did when she thought of her sister, but it wasn't there. She ran her hand around her neck, over her collarbones, and up under her hair. She felt around down the front and the back of her shirt. Her necklace was most definitely gone. Had she forgotten to put it back on after her morning swim? It was then her probing fingers encountered one loose end of the chain caught in the fine hairs, which escaped her braid at the back of her head. She gently tugged the chain free. Suddenly, she remembered her braid catching on something when she was back in the engine room. God, where was her pendant now? What if someone saw it and realized she was on board?

Then again, who could recognize it as hers?

She fixated on these uncertainties, though there was absolutely nothing she could do about them. She had achieved her goal, she was out on Escalle's yacht during one of its nightly jaunts. Now what should she do?

She couldn't exactly stroll out on the deck and see what was afoot. Such an appearance wouldn't bode well for her longevity. She cursed her own lack of planning. She had been so focused on getting on board she hadn't put a great deal of thought into what would happen when she'd successfully done so. She had had some idea of finding a hiding place that would allow her to either observe or overhear the activities on the upper decks. As it turned out, she was buried down in this bathroom with no possibility of seeing or hearing anything.

All of a sudden, the *Calypso's* engines went quiet. It was utterly still in her bathroom. She strained to hear any sounds, but the yacht remained agonizingly silent. More time passed, fifteen or twenty minutes since the engine had been shut off. Unsure if she was imagining things, she thought she heard footsteps. A door slammed shut. The footsteps sounded like they were coming closer. They stopped again. She reached into her bag, searching for some weapon. Why hadn't she brought her second gun?

Where was her knife? She was such an idiot or, rather, such a complete amateur. She grasped the handle of the heavy flashlight.

As she heard the door to the bunkroom from the corridor open, she tried to stand up. Pins and needles shot through her legs, which had been bent in an awkward position for so long. They crumpled beneath her. As she fell, she involuntarily grabbed the shower curtain, which tore as it came down with her. She banged her head on the plastic lining of the stall, then struggled to get free of the enveloping plastic. Achingly bright neon lights came on. Skylar squinted against the cruelly white light, and jerked the curtain off her head. She gritted her teeth against the shooting pains in her legs. She looked for something to grab onto, so that she could pull herself upright.

"Hello, Skylar." Luke remarked calmly. He reached down to offer her his hand.

She grasped it willingly, and allowed him to pull her to her feet. Once there, she leaned against the wall, regrouping and allowing the circulation to resume in her legs.

"Luke, thank goodness it's you! I was so scared. I didn't know who—"

"You're right, you didn't know, did you? What do you think you're

135

doing here? You never give up, do you? You came to search the *Calypso*. Escalle is not a stupid man. This yacht is completely clean. I make sure she is when we return to port or whenever there is a good chance we might be getting a visit from Customs and Border Protection. The only time this yacht is ever involved in anything remotely illegal is when she is safely far out on International Waters."

"I just wanted to see."

He grinned. The sardonic smile did nothing to soften his antagonistic demeanor. "You and your sister are birds of a feather. I found her hiding behind the island in the kitchen."

"You found Maia?"

"Yeah, I did. I've never denied it. Can you stand on your own now? Give it a second, and then we'll head upstairs. I could use a drink."

"What did you do to Maia?"

"I chopped her up into bite-sized pieces and threw her overboard for the sharks." He chuckled. "I thought you had a good sense of humor. I'm kidding. You still think I may have killed her, don't you? You're unbelievable, lady."

"You just said…"

"I said I found her. Then, I contacted my boss. A boat met us, and picked your sister up. Since then, she's been hidden at a safe location. She's in the Witness Protection Program. Maia is very much alive. You ready?"

She nodded, having a hard time processing this incredible revelation. "She's really okay?"

"Yeah. Let's go." He waited until she had wobbled past him on her stiff legs. He shut off the light, closed the door, and followed her through the bunkroom, and then up the steps.

With a large hand pressed gently but firmly against the small of her back, he piloted her back into the main salon, where he went straight to the bar. He poured himself some Jack Daniel's, straight, and swallowed it down. "Couldn't you have found a better hiding place than the crew head?"

"Head? Oh, you mean the bathroom. Well, I would have found something more comfortable except then I heard voices. I didn't have enough time to be selective. Who else is on board?"

"No one. Some of the guys were helping me before we got underway, but they all stayed on shore. What would you like to drink?" he questioned, as he dropped ice into two empty cocktail glasses.

"A Diet Coke."

"Have some bourbon with your Coke. You'll feel better."

"I'm not a real bourbon fan, but right now it sounds good."

He finished mixing the simple drinks, and handed her one. She was leaning up against the bar, loathe to sit again and inflict further abuse on her cramped limbs. He stood overly close to her. He looked straight into her eyes, obviously trying to establish control through body language and sheer physical intimidation. "So what do I have to do to keep you from blowing this operation?"

Rather than being unsettled, she found that she was becoming turned on. Because she was tall and very fit, she had always found most men disappointingly soft and feminine. Luke was straight alpha male from his broad shoulders to the muscular thighs dusted with tawny hair revealed by his cut-off shorts.

She grasped her glass and took a gulp. The bourbon barely diluted with cold coke burned a path down her throat. "I'm not trying to screw anything up, but you never really gave me any straight answers before. If you had just told me the truth, I would have left it alone. Hell, I probably would have done what you wanted me to do and just left."

"I don't believe that for a second. You still would have put your pretty, little nose where it shouldn't be. You may be willing to sell yourself, but you are persistent."

"Look, you have this all wrong. I was never going to be Escalle's..." She paused, searching for the right word.

"Bitch?" he supplied with a cocked, blond eyebrow.

"Concubine. I didn't think he meant it until Lillian said something about redecorating Yvette's bedroom. I intended to avoid giving him an answer for as long as I could, to prolong my stay at Casa del Mar. Otherwise, I have to leave in two weeks."

"Well, that's good news." He moved closer to her, like a large, predatory cat eyeing a tasty prey.

She tossed back some more of her stiff drink, and found the noxious stuff went down smoother when she didn't really taste it, but merely swallowed. "How did you figure out that I was on board? Are there cameras somewhere?"

"No. Martin is too smart a guy to make hard copies of anything that takes place on this yacht. I knew you were on board because of this." He took her hand and drew it toward his waistband.

"Whoa. Slow down. We have to talk right now."

"My pocket, sugar. Reach into my pocket."

Despite her better judgment, she allowed those long, tan fingers to guide hers into the soft cotton material. She delved for a moment. Then, she encountered a hard, metal object. She pulled it out. She stared at the familiar shape of a sterling silver dolphin jumping through a white gold hoop. "I knew I'd lost it. It got caught in my hair and I jerked it."

"I found it down below," he said. "Actually, Hank found it when we were putting in some supplies. You lucked out in that I happened to be with him when he found it. I told him it was mine. None of those guys knew it was yours. They've never really been physically close to you. Bill was up on top. He might have recognized it, but I don't think he heard anything about it."

"I don't think he would recognize it if he had. He doesn't strike me as the most observant guy."

"Don't sell him short. He's not stupid."

"Do you really think he would notice what sort of necklace I wear?"

He reached out and ran his fingertip along her jaw line. "I did."

"Yes, but you…You've been a lot closer to me," she sputtered. All of the fear and anxiety of the past few hours melted into something thick, hot, and wicked in her core. She was suddenly aware her nipples felt very sensitive and alive.

"That's true." His voice had gone deeper and more velvety. He leaned closer to her. His eyes were hot and hungry, and all over Skylar. "Of course, I'm always trying to get a peek down your shirt."

Involuntarily, she took a step back and found herself pressed up against the cool, smooth wood of the bar. "I thought you were angry with me, that you believed I was getting involved with Escalle."

He allowed his long, solid length to brush up against her body. "I've been thinking, sweetheart. You weren't planning on moving in with the guy, were you?"

"No, absolutely not. That's what I've been trying to tell you. I didn't want to tell him 'No' until right before I planned to leave."

"That's what I figured. I would have done the same. It's just that thinking about you with Martin, it got me all hot and bothered. A different kind of hot and bothered than I am right now." His lip curled up in that sexy half smile that had an immediate and devastating impact on her senses.

Skylar recognized she was drowning, fast. She grasped for straws. "So, just like that, you're not mad at me, everything is okay? Just like that?" she squeaked.

"You were worried about your sister. I can't blame you for that." He gripped the bar on either side of her, leaning in to her. She was aware of his spicy, tropical cologne mingled with a hint of Jack Daniel's, and his unique male scent. She was a grown woman, she reminded herself, a woman who knew what she wanted and went after it, or, in this case, him. She definitely wanted Luke White, here and now, with her pulse throbbing within her, and her body electrically responsive to his every move, his every breath. She placed her hands low on his waist and slid them up slowly, deliberately until they draped around his neck.

He responded aggressively to her blatant invitation. His velvety lips were upon hers seeking and demanding her response. She held nothing back. She opened beneath him, and suckled his tongue into her mouth. He kissed her hungrily.

She was completely lost in him, blind to her surroundings, caught up in the erotic feel and promise of the moment and of this man. There was no hurry to his seduction. He savored her, gentled her lips with his own, and then slowly built up the heat and the passion. His kiss and his touch wove a powerful sensual spell. But then he drew back away from her.

"Skylar, I want you."

Chapter Sixteen

His expression was enough to send a nun running in fear. To her, he looked like a golden-haired Viking god of passion, way too much man for any woman to walk away from.

Skylar had no intention of doing so. It felt like she'd waited her whole life for a man to look at her in just this way. She desired him with every fiber of her being. She knew she would shrivel up and die if she didn't have him soon. She focused on these sensations, determinedly ignoring the little voice in her head that argued she felt far more than lust for Luke White.

"So, what do you say?"

"Don't stop." Her voice sounded throaty to her own ears.

She thought she heard something that sounded distinctly like a growl before she felt those large, warm hands grasp the neckline of her T-shirt. She gasped in pleased, heated surprise as he ripped her shirt in two. For the barest moment, she was embarrassed that she was wearing a black sports bra, instead of sexy lingerie. She reached under her breasts to yank it off.

He groaned. Hot, hungry hands moved up over her ribs to cup her breasts. She pressed into his palms.

"I've dreamed about this for so long, and when it finally happens, I would be wearing a sports bra."

"Underwear has never been my thing. I'd much rather see you out of it...Um, perfect." He circled one dusky nipple with the edge of his thumb. It grew taut and puckered in response. His hands continued to caress her, to learn her. He pulled her back against him, and nuzzled her neck and the delicate, sensitive place behind her ear. "That poster didn't do you justice, and I thought you were *smokin'* back then."

"I thought it was your roommate's poster."

"It was, but I think both of us jerked off looking at it."

She laughed. "My coach would have been thrilled to know that. He thought the article and the pictures would motivate girls to participate in swimming. I really don't think he intended to provide inspiration to horny college boys."

"Sugar, you were a fantasy for me then, and you most definitely are now. I always wanted to reach into that poster and grab this butt of yours." He gripped her rump with both hands.

The combination of irreverent humor and genuine wonder was the most potent aphrodisiac for Skylar. Her world became concentrated into the feeling of this man against her, her own raging desire, and the need to get the rest of her clothing off as quickly as possible.

He picked her up. She wrapped her long legs around him. She continued to kiss him, her mouth, open, hungry and demanding. He began to walk. She didn't care where he was taking her as long as it was close by. He set her down on the edge of the pool table.

He stood cradled between her legs. In a quick move, he jerked his T-shirt up over his head. His chest was a broad expanse of sun-burnished skin. Light brown hair dusted his high, firm pecs and trailed down the middle of his stomach, bisecting his defined abdominal muscles. His skin felt scorchingly hot to her touch. When she ran her fingers over the flat, hard surface of his belly, he sucked in air.

She reached for his waistband, eager to slide his shorts down and reveal what lay beneath. Their eyes met as he retreated for a moment. She tilted forward, pursuing him. Her fingers slid under the elastic. His penis was silky smooth, exactly the right thickness, and big. She shoved the shorts down.

"I want to see you. To taste you."

He let her have her way with him. He was tall enough that she had only to bend at the waist to get close to his cock. She reached out, cupping him. With her other hand, she manipulated his soft but heavy testicles. He tensed. Aware his eyes were upon her, she extended the tip of her tongue, and lathed the head of his manhood. He shivered in response.

"You have a perfect penis."

"I'm certainly glad you think so," he muttered.

She slowly slid her mouth down to the base of his penis, taking his shaft deep into her throat.

"Oh my God."

She continued to massage his balls, and then used her own saliva to lubricate the movement of her hand and mouth on his penis.

"That's right. Suck me and jerk me off like that, baby… You're so good."

She continued her actions until she felt his large hands grip her own. "Whoa. Stop. It's my turn." He pressed her down so that she lay flat on the pool table. He gently tugged her by the hips so that her bottom projected over the edge. He tugged her sweat pants down her hips, revealing her black bikini underwear. These he disposed of as well. He kissed and stroked his way up from her toes to her calves, and up her thighs. Initially, she felt very exposed and vulnerable. But she quickly relaxed under the waves of sensation. She drew her legs up and braced her feet against the wooden rim of the table.

"So sweet. You taste so good," he crooned as he breathed into her womanhood, and rubbed his stubbled cheeks against her labia. "Hot damn, you shave. A sexy, little, dark strip."

She had always trimmed her pubic hair into a tight line because of the variety of swimming suits she wore. Still she was glad she had done so the night before, so the trim job was tight and neat and her skin, smooth and soft. Then, his tongue danced across her clitoris, and all thought left her. She pressed the heel of her hand into her mouth and bit down.

His tongue and lips nuzzled her, tortured her, devastated her. She dug her fingers into his hair. It was too good. Too much. She arched her hips up, pressing his face closer, his tongue, deeper.

"I'm going to come…Wait. I mean. Please, I want to come with you. Do you have any condoms?"

He grinned at her, and reached into his pocket. He pulled out a foil wrapped packet. He tore the corner open with his teeth. He slid it smoothly down over his penis. "I grabbed them from Angelique's stateroom after I found the pendant. I thought maybe I'd get lucky."

"Shut up." It was her turn to grab him by his buns as she sat up. He shoved straight into her as their lips met. She gasped as he filled her, stretched her. In her mouth, his tongue mimicked the motion of his cock. He braced himself with one hand and with the other, took hers. He led her fingers down to where they were joined.

"Touch yourself," he directed against her lips. "It turns me on."

She willingly obeyed him. She reached down between them and began to manipulate her clitoris. Soon, they were straining against each other. She met his thrusts with her own.

"Harder! Yes! Oh... Please." She melted away into a sea of exploding, iridescent bubbles of sensation, but it didn't stop there. He was straining toward his own orgasm, his rhythm becoming more frantic, his motion, wilder. Then, he drove into her mercilessly, burying himself to the hilt. He groaned as both of them came together.

They lay still, allowing the waves of wonder to wash over them and then, slowly, fade away. She felt a warm drop of sweat slip from his side onto her.

He raised his head slowly. "I don't think I've ever done it on a pool table, even in college."

"God, that was good," she murmured, still loathe to move.

"I generally try to have the sexual history talk before I fuck the hell out of someone."

"I find that wise," she agreed as she ran her fingers up over the firm lines of his back and butt. "I'm trying to decide whether that felt so amazing because of how long it's been for me, or because you really are as good as you think you are."

He tilted back and withdrew from her body. Then, he leaned forward to nuzzle her neck. "Honey, I really am that good. Give me a minute and I'll give you another demonstration."

"*Mmmm...* That sounds fabulous." She reached down between them and grasped his testicles. She gently cupped the warm, heavy flesh. His penis began to respond almost immediately.

"Let's take this somewhere more comfortable." He hoisted his shorts up over his narrow hips. Then, he scooped her up in his arms. He was halfway to the door when he paused. "I forgot something."

"My clothes?"

"No, the drinks. Can you grab them?"

"Yeah...I think. Got 'em. If you put me down, I can get my clothes, too."

"Not a chance. I like you better this way, naked and at my mercy. We're the only two people on board the *Calypso*. Your clothes are fine where they are. Besides, I'm getting a kick out of sweeping you off your feet. It appeals to my macho nature."

"All right, Tarzan," she grinned. It was a rather delicious and novel sensation, being hefted about as if she weighed no more than doll.

"Want to try out the master suite?"

"Escalle's room? That's kind of weird, don't you think?"

"I don't know. It seemed like you were headed that way for a while."

"Oh, come on." She rolled her eyes in exasperation. "I already explained all of that."

"Hey, I was only kidding. Watch the drinks. This one's usually Angelique's. It has mirrors in some pretty wild places."

"You would know."

He grinned and snuggled her close, but bypassed this second doorway. He nipped on her earlobe. She shivered in sexual anticipation. He paused outside a third doorway and fumbled with the door handle.

"If you would just put me down."

"No chance." He used his foot to push the door wide. He flipped the light switch on. They were in a well-appointed guest suite. He laid her down on the bed. As he moved around the room, she ogled his body appreciatively. He fiddled with a panel of switches by the door, allowing her an unrestricted view of a very muscular back. He discreetly illuminated the room by adjusting the power of the recessed track lighting on the ceiling. Just audible classical music began to play from some wall-mounted speakers.

Skylar recognized the piece as Beethoven's Moonlight Sonata. She glanced up at Luke in some surprise.

"I'm a Parrot head, myself, but you're a very classy lady. Beethoven's kind of sexy, don't you think? Besides, there's only classical music on this CD player." He leered at her as he dropped his shorts and kicked them away. She nearly groaned aloud. The man was spectacularly built and fully aroused. Like a golden cat, he slowly, decadently extended himself down on the bed, covering her body with his own.

"I haven't been able to stop thinking about you."

She kissed him back hungrily. Her passion rose instantly to meet his. They touched, stroked, and caressed. His hands slid down to her wrists. He drew them slowly up over her head. Holding them there with one hand, and pinning the rest of her down with his heavy legs and body, he began to play with one of her nipples. At the same time, he rubbed his hot and swollen cock against the juncture of her legs. She moaned.

"We have to talk," he announced. He continued to knead her nipples, but his eyes met her own disbelieving ones.

"Now?" she demanded incredulously.

"Skylar, I want to explain something to you. I haven't been with anyone in quite a while because I'm working on a case. I don't get involved with women when I'm working. Do you understand what I'm telling you?"

She squashed down her immediate sense of dismay. So, he was only after physical gratification. If that was the case, it was better she knew it now. Fool, she berated herself. She had already been thinking red roses and white picket fences. She pinched her eyes shut against the tears, which threatened to spill over.

She was a big girl. She should know better.

"Hey, sugar, what's wrong?"

She turned her face away from him. Ignoring him proved difficult when he extended one long arm down between them. His fingers stroked and teased her clitoris. She bucked beneath him. He was working a wet and wonderful magic on her.

"What do you see happening here? With us?"

One finger dipped in between the folds of her labia. She wanted more, now, immediately. She nearly whimpered in aggravation. She struggled against him, but found that both frustrating and arousing. She couldn't break away; he was too strong. And, in all honesty, she didn't really want to be free.

"Tell me," he demanded, increasing his torment. Just when she was about to come, he stopped.

"Luke, please!"

"Tell me how you feel."

"Fine." She spit out. She had always been the direct sort. "You might as well know. I'm more than a little in love with you," she admitted. "I promise I won't bother you when this is all over. If you don't want us to keep seeing each other, I'll go away."

He silenced her by sliding back up over her body. "Shh."

He began to kiss her again, and his penis nudged her belly. He was taking his time, savoring her.

"Sweetheart, that's just what I wanted to hear. Of course, I want to see you when all this is done. Didn't you hear what I just told you? I don't get involved with women during an investigation, but I did with you.

"We're right together. I needed to hear you had feelings for me, too. I know I'm rushing you, and we should be getting to know each other. I should be romancing you, but there isn't time. I can't let you keep putting yourself in danger. So, for right now, all we have is tonight… That'll change. I'm planning on making it through this. I wanted you to know you're special to me. I wouldn't be here now with you if you weren't."

She was deeply touched by how open and expressive this strong, decent man was being with her. She sensed that he was floundering now. It was her turn to whisper *"Shhh."* It was her turn to stroke and then grasp his penis, and slide the condom down over it.

"Let me finish. I'm thirty-one, I'm just a regular guy. I don't have much except a sailboat I'm refitting, but I want you, and I don't only mean for now."

She smiled coyly at him. "I want you, too. Right now. Come on, cowboy." She rolled over onto her stomach invitingly.

Looking at him over her shoulder, she saw his already impressive erection grew larger still. In the space of a heartbeat, he was gripping her hips.

"God, yes!" He plunged fully into her. They both nearly came apart at the sensation.

For Skylar, it proved to be a timeless, miraculous night. They talked, made love, and ultimately fell asleep wrapped in each other's arms.

* * * *

Skylar awoke first as the soft, pastel lights of the dawn began to penetrate the stateroom. In repose, Luke's stubbled face was gentler, younger, more innocent. She longed to reach out and touch him, but she didn't want to wake him, not yet.

Carefully, she drew back away from him, extracting her limbs from his. He muttered something incomprehensible, but his eyes remained closed. His tanned, muscular frame stood out against the snowy, silky sheets. He looked delicious, and it all felt so new and exciting. She paused, savoring the sensation.

Then, she shivered in the cool, morning sea air. The hair on her arms stood upright as she hastened into the bathroom. She was looking forward to getting back into bed and snuggling up to that very warm, very male body.

She flipped the lights. A fan began to discreetly hum. She attended to her needs. Then, she washed her hands, and peered into the mirror before her. Her features were the same as always, but her cheeks and her chin were rosy from rubbing against his stubble. Her eyes were overly bright and large with fatigue. She touched her fingertips to the purple shadows below them. She smiled. Neither of them had gotten much sleep.

She loved him! There was no way to foretell what the future might bring. But she couldn't resist imagining the years unfolding before them, years spent together. All of that would have to wait until Escalle was brought to justice, until Maia could return to her normal life.

"Skylar? Skylar, where are you?" His voice was deep and sleep-roughened.

"I'll be right out."

"I kept your spot warm," he purred through the door.

She hit the lights and was back in bed in a matter of seconds.

Chapter Seventeen

It was almost noon when they finally emerged from the bed. They were both famished. After an erotic, shared shower, they made their way to the galley. There, Luke worked on scrambling eggs, while Skylar manned the toaster and coffeemaker.

"You want the Swiss cheese or the American?" she asked as she peered into the refrigerator. She was wearing a white 'wife beater' T-shirt and candy cane striped boxer shorts that she borrowed from Luke. He had on a bright yellow T-shirt that advertised a Key West watering hole and a pair of well-worn, drawstring shorts. Both were barefoot.

"I like the Swiss. That okay with you?"

"Sounds good. Who taught you how to cook?"

"My mother made sure my brother and I could feed ourselves before we left home. It's come in handy." He grinned at her. "Chicks are always really impressed when a guy can make a decent breakfast for them."

"I'm sure you've had a lot of practice then," she remarked dryly.

"It's one of the many skills I've honed over the years. But don't be jealous, you're the only lady I want to scramble eggs for now."

"Give me a break," she chuckled. "You're impossible. Do you want butter on your toast?"

"Butter and raspberry jam. If you really want to impress me, you can cut the crusts off my bread."

"You're kidding, right?"

"My mother does."

"Did she peel your grapes, too?"

"Actually, she did."

"My mother warned me about Mama's boys."

148

"What did she say?

"That you can never win if you're competing with a woman for her son. So, I'll leave the grapes and crusts to your mother. I wouldn't want to tread on her toes."

He laughed. "My mom is going to love you. When this is all over, I'd like you to meet her." He paused, scooping mountains of eggs onto plates. "Have you ever been snorkeling?"

"Yes, in the Bahamas. I was at a swim meet there, and I went snorkeling with my friends. It was a blast."

"Sweetheart, in about ten minutes, we can be at the National Marine Sanctuary. It's like another world down there. You'll love it."

"I thought you had to scuba dive to see the reefs."

"That's true in some places, but not here. Skin-diving we probably won't see any sea turtles or nurse sharks, but I'm in the mood for something lazy that doesn't require too much concentration. You float along while you're snorkeling, check out the fish and the coral. Unwind. The colors are really spectacular. You game?"

"Yeah, it sounds great…Oh, no! I left a note for Cole that if I didn't make it back by tonight to go to the authorities."

"What did you think I was going to do to you?"

She could see by his expression that he was only half joking. "I knew that you were one of the good guys. I wanted to cover my bases. I wasn't sure you would be taking the yacht out alone. I know that some nights you have other people onboard. No, I knew you weren't the big bad wolf."

"Oh, kinky. I've always had a thing for little Red Riding Hood. Would you wear a red cape for me some time? So I can gobble you up?"

"You already did that, but I'm up for another round."

He pulled her against him, nipped at her lips, then buried his face against the side of her neck. "Woman, consider it a promise, as long as you reciprocate."

In answer, she reached down and stroked him through the thin material of his shorts. "You've got a deal."

They lost themselves in another soul-draining kiss. Luke was the one who pulled back first. "Slow down, sweetheart. If you really want to get back by this afternoon, we have to get going. By the way, what else did you tell Cole?"

"Nothing else. Just to watch for me and go to the authorities if I don't show up."

"Damn, Skylar. Why didn't you talk to me about this? I don't trust him."

"He's a good guy, Luke. He seems to really care about Maia. He has her picture up in his room."

"I know he had the hots for her, but I don't think she reciprocated. They went out a few times. Then, she sort of blew him off."

"Maia mentioned meeting someone down here in her e-mails to me."

"How do you know the guy was Cole? Before she left, she was involved with another guy, actually a Customs and Immigration officer. She went to him with her suspicions, and from what I understand, they hit it off. We really had to hose him down when we placed her in the program."

"I didn't know about any of this. Is there some way we can contact Maia?"

"Honey, I don't know where she is, or even who she is for that matter right now. It's better that way, for her safety."

"This doesn't necessarily make Cole a bad guy." Her words didn't sound convincing even to her own ears.

"Did you know that he sometimes works as a personal assistant to Escalle?"

She felt rather ill. "I really blew it. He'll go straight to Escalle."

"That's my guess."

"What can we do? Your investigation, Luke, I'm so sorry. I've ruined everything."

"Actually, I think we're okay. Cole will go to his boss, but that doesn't mean we're totally sunk. Escalle has been suspicious of you for some time, ever since Bill caught you in the library. Escalle told all of us to keep an eye on you. I don't think he was too concerned about you. He kept you around."

"He just fired me."

"Yeah, because he has a big deal going down."

"Then why would he jeopardize it by asking me to stay on as his mistress?"

"For three reasons, because he is taken with you, he thinks he can control you, and he underestimates you. Women are the only area in his life where I have observed Martin Escalle being careless or impulsive. Of course, he generally has the last word when it comes to women. Remember poor Yvette."

"You think he killed her."

"I think her death was very convenient, but back to Cole. Don't worry about him. He won't contact anyone. He'll wait to see what I do, and I'll tell them the truth. That I discovered you on board, and then I spent all night screwing your brains out. That's something they're sure to understand. Don't worry. So let's go snorkeling. We'll still be back in plenty of time. "

He reached out and took her hand. He squeezed it, and then drew it up to his lips. Delicately, he ran his tongue in between her fingers. She shivered in response, and moved to press her body against his. Her sensitive breasts were flattened against his hard chest. She could feel his impressive erection through the thin layers of clothing between them. He slid his hands under her shorts.

"No undies. How sexy and convenient," he murmured, before taking her lips with his own. He growled, untying his shorts, and guiding her toward the countertop.

About twenty minutes later, they were underway. Luke was in the pilothouse, and Skylar sat out on the deck, sipping her coffee and enjoying the feel of the sun on her skin and the wind in her hair. It was one of those spectacular, gloriously clear, eighty-five degree, Key West days when there truly is nowhere else in the world more beautiful.

She felt supremely relaxed and peaceful. For a few more hours, she wouldn't think about her problems. She intended to enjoy every moment of this stolen day with a glorious, golden man. In way too short a time for her, they had arrived at their destination. The air seemed strangely quiet and still when Luke shut off the engine. The *Calypso* gently rocked in the aquamarine waters.

"We're here," he announced. "You see where the water is a lighter green over there?" He pointed.

"Where?" She shaded her eyes with her hand, and peered out. She couldn't make out any differences in the water.

"Right there. Do you see that seagull? Now look a little to the right."

"Yes. Yes, I see it. That whole area's a different color."

"That's the reef. We'll swim from here. We don't want to get any closer and risk damaging it."

"You want to swim all the way out there?"

"Come on," he teased. "That's barely a couple of laps in the pool. Nothing to an Olympian." He wrapped his arms around her and pulled her close. She leaned into him. "Remember the night you swam out to the *Calypso*? She was half-a-mile out, and it was getting dark."

"Yes, but I wasn't up the whole night before."

"That wasn't my fault. I distinctly remember you waking me up that last time. It'll be really easy going with the flippers. The water will feel great. Trust me. The snorkeling equipment is stored below. I'll be right back."

A few minutes later, he was back on deck carrying a green, plastic tub. He opened it up, and tossed a few masks and snorkels out.

"I know Angelique's gear is in here somewhere," he muttered.

"Ew. I don't use anything that's been in her mouth."

He paused in his rummaging and raised his eyebrows at her over his sunglasses. "We disinfect everything before we put it away. It's all sanitary. This should fit." He handed her a mask and a snorkel. "What size are your feet?"

"Nine."

"These'll work. They're men's sevens, but they should be about right."

Shortly thereafter, she slid off the swimming deck into the water wearing her black sports bra and matching underwear as well as the snorkeling gear. Luke was already swimming along ahead of her. She felt her energy level rising as she began to pursue him. It took her no time at all to get reacquainted with the snorkeling gear. She was kicking along steadily, partially submerged. Her movements appeared graceful and languid underwater. Even though they were not yet to the reef, she found herself mesmerized by the aquatic world.

Ahead of her, Luke paused. He waited for her to catch up. He pointed to the surface. They kicked their way up, spitting out their mouthpieces.

"We're almost there. You're going to love it, sweetheart. But don't touch anything. The ecosystem on the reef is very delicate."

"You stopped us here to tell me that?" she sputtered as she treaded water.

"Sorry. It's just that this is kind of a special place for me. I come out here whenever I need a break from the investigation or time to think. I'm really going to miss it when all of this is done."

Over his shoulder, she observed a sailboat in the distance. Then, she glimpsed a red speedboat moving rapidly in their direction. She could make out the hum of its powerful engine over the sounds of lapping water. She nodded toward the speedboat, which was still pretty far away but was showing no signs of slowing down. "We aren't going to be run over, are we?"

"Boats aren't allowed out over the reef. It's against the law," he reassured her. "You ready?"

"Yup." She pulled the mask back down over her eyes and gave him the thumbs up.

They floated along the top of the water, gently using their flippers to push them forward. Sunlight easily penetrated the shallow emerald water, revealing the magical and completely alien world of the reef.

Skylar had been snorkeling before, in the Bahamas, but that rather monochromatic, unexciting experience had not prepared her for this visual feast. There were all sorts of brightly colored tropical fish darting in and out of sight through the labyrinthine coral. She identified star coral and sea fans from some long forgotten Jacques Cousteau special. She saw angelfish and a pair of barracuda darting about. But, for the most part, the reef was completely foreign to her, with its brilliant shades of pink, green, and blue, its darting, silver schools of fish, and its curious-looking invertebrates.

They stayed side-by-side, taking turns pointing out sights and creatures. She lost all sense of time. She also completely forgot how tired she was, the experience was so fascinating, so overwhelming.

Eventually, Luke gripped her hand, and they broke through the surface together.

"Did you see that lobster?" he asked, grinning like a kid as he flipped his mask back.

"It was huge."

"I should have brought a net."

"I thought you can't take anything from the reef." It was her turn to tease.

"You can't take the irreplaceable stuff, like the coral. There's no problem with taking a lobster, as long as you're careful."

"It's just as well. Putting a living creature in boiling water gives me the creeps."

"They're delicious, and it's no crueler than eating a hamburger or a steak."

"I don't have to kill the cow, or watch it get killed. Give me a break. I know I'm a hypocrite."

He raised his forearm and peered at his diving watch. "Skylar, we've been out here for more than an hour. It'll take us another half hour to get back to the yacht. We should head back."

She made no attempt to mask her dismay. "I could stay out here all day."

"We'll do this again, sweetheart, but from my boat, the *Betty Grable*."

With that promise filling her heart, she pressed the mouthpiece back into her mouth. They swam slowly but steadily in the direction from which they had come. Before long, they were off the reef and proceeding toward the *Calypso*.

They were in the open water, about halfway between the reef and the yacht when Skylar surfaced to clean out her goggles. She had gotten some water in them, and her vision was obscured. She pulled them off, and immediately noticed that a small, white boat with an outboard motor was secured to the much larger yacht. A thrill of pure fear coursed through her as she observed two dark, male figures moving around on the deck. They were still too far away to make their identity out. She swam frantically after Luke. She caught up with him and clutched his arm.

He surfaced. His back was to the *Calypso*. He grinned at her. "You feeling frisky? I haven't done it in the ocean since high school, but what the hell."

"Look! Get down!" But it was already too late. One of the shadowed figures pointed directly at them. Skylar watched in horror as the other one raised and aimed a rifle.

Chapter Eighteen

Skylar watched the man with the gun in horror.

Luke yelled, "Swim! Don't look back. We have to split up. That way it'll be harder to target us."

"But..."

"Now!" He pushed her under. She choked on salty seawater, but managed to stay down. Under water, he pointed in the direction of the distant shore. He mouthed, "Swim!"

She understood. She swam as far as she could on her half breath. She surfaced for only a second and then dove deep again. She correctly assumed the depths offered her greater protection. She dared not use her snorkel. She guessed that it would be visible if the rifleman had a scope on his gun.

She concentrated desperately on breathing, kicking, and pulling the water behind her, trying to regain the single-minded focus of her competition days, but her mind was already occupied with thoughts of Luke. Was he all right? Or, was he...?

No, she had to believe he was alive.

For an endless fifteen or twenty minutes, she continued the frantic race for survival. She knew she was a good distance from her starting point, but still far from the shore. She wanted to take a quick look, and see what was going on. She hesitated for only a second and then swam to the surface. With her heart pounding, she shoved her head out, and then back under the water. The first time she did it, she saw nothing. Cautiously, she swam a little further. This time, as she surfaced, she glimpsed a flash of red. The speedboat she had seen earlier was now right beside the yacht. Several people were moving around on the deck of the yacht.

Was this some sort of rendezvous at sea? It seemed rather bold to her that it would take place in the middle of the afternoon.

She dived again. There wasn't much chance she could evade them if they sought her out in the faster, smaller craft. She was a small target, but with binoculars, a scope, and patience, both she and Luke could be located easily enough. Besides, she couldn't play this game forever. It was simply a matter of time. She set out for the shore once more. It was her only chance.

She was heading up for air when someone or something grabbed her ankle, pulling her back down. Her straining lungs protested. She fought desperately, blindly. Strong arms encircled her. In a moment of clarity, she recognized she wasn't going to be shot. Instead, she was going to be drowned.

Suddenly, she found herself being irresistibly dragged up, up to the radiance of air and sunlight. Gasping and choking, she inhaled eagerly and found herself staring into Luke's brown eyes.

She stopped fighting and wrapped her arms around his neck. Unfortunately, this sudden change in her behavior caused his head to plunge back under the water. He came back up snorting and choking. Once he cleared the salt water from his nose and mouth, he proved to be laughing.

"I manage to catch up with you, and then you try to drown me."

"I didn't realize it was you."

"I figured that."

"We should keep swimming. They might see us. I thought you said we were safer apart." The words burst out of her in staccato.

"We're okay now. They took off. You see that speedboat? It's Coast Guard. I have no idea what they're doing out here. They probably stopped at the *Calypso* to harass me. There's an officer named Robertson who is suspicious of me and of Escalle. He doesn't know I'm undercover. He's searched the *Calypso* before, just to be a prick. I'll have to send him a thank you when this is all over. We lucked out."

"Where do you think they went?" She was referring to the shooter and his accomplice.

"They left in their boat when they saw the Coast Guard vessel heading in their direction. They're probably back at shore by now."

"Thank God."

"Yeah. Robertson is a pain in the ass, but I'm really glad to see him today. Come on. Let's get back. Unlike you, I'm not used to swimming this far. I'm getting pretty tired out here."

"How very un-macho of you. Actually, I'm impressed you managed to keep up with me."

"Hey, it wasn't easy. I lost you a couple of times. Then I saw you surface a few minutes ago. I knew you were making for the shore, and so I guessed I might be able to intercept you over here. I'm just glad you slowed down for a few minutes there. It's hard to catch a mermaid in her element."

"Do you think those guys will come back?"

"Not now, with Robertson on patrol. It would look suspicious if we were to disappear now. Still, it was pretty ballsy for them to take shots at us in broad daylight."

"What if they did something to the *Calypso*?"

"I always knew you're a clever girl. I don't think they had enough time. I'll check her over, but I don't think Bill would know how to sabotage her."

"Bill Stevens? How do you know it was him?"

"His build. He has a weightlifter's stance and strut. I'm pretty sure he was our sniper. He's a good shot. We're lucky to be alive. I've gotta admit I'm surprised. Bill is not a proactive guy. This was an unusually bold move for him. I'm not sure who the other guy in the baseball cap was. I just wonder…" His voice trailed off.

"What?"

"Nothing."

"Just say it."

"All right." He cocked an eyebrow at her. "I was wondering if they were after you or me."

"That's a happy thought."

"Maybe they didn't want to kill us, merely scare us, or you."

"If that was their intent, they succeeded admirably."

"I'll race you back." He grinned cheekily.

"Are you going to tell this Coast Guard officer about Bill?"

"We're not going to tell him anything. While we were snorkeling, some friends came out to the *Calypso* and missed us. That's all."

"You mean we're going to go back to Casa del Mar as if nothing happened?"

"Yes, sweetheart. Trust me. I'll meet you back at the yacht."

She set off in her powerful crawl. This was her strongest, most efficient stroke. It ate up the distance. She concentrated on breathing and swimming, not on what lay ahead.

As expected, Robertson greeted them at the swimming platform. He was a ruddy-faced, heavy set, middle-aged fellow who was flushed and splotchy from the heat, but there was a shrewdness to his blue eyes that belied his sloppy appearance. Luke told him his story, and then willingly took him on an inspection of the yacht. The dissatisfied officer eventually left after giving Luke the rather heavy-handed warning that, "He would be watching him."

Luke waited for the other man to depart. Then, he started the engines and headed the *Calypso* back to shore.

Skylar joined him up in the pilothouse. He was sitting in the black leather captain's chair studying the overhead electronics console.

"What a day," she offered.

"Yeah." He swallowed. "Look, Skylar, I'm serious about this. I want you to leave tonight."

"No. I'm not leaving."

"Things could get very ugly. I don't want any civilians getting in the way."

"There are other 'civilians' at Casa del Mar."

"But I don't…I don't want to see anything happen to you." Without taking his eyes from the water, he reached out and pulled her firmly against him. He leaned down and kissed her forehead.

"I want to be with you for the long haul, which I think we would both prefer to extend beyond tonight. I want you to promise me that, when we get back, you'll leave immediately. As quickly as possible. Don't say anything specific to anyone, just pack up and go. I want us to get out of this mess alive. It'll make my job a lot easier if I don't have to worry about you, too."

"Okay," she agreed quietly.

"Look, it's all going to be over with soon…What? You mean that you'll go?"

"I can see that I'll be in the way. Promise me you'll take care of yourself."

"Escalle's Columbian deal is set to go down in the next few weeks, if not days. Then, I think he's going to try and leave the country. He has more than enough money in offshore accounts to go now, but he's being greedy. He wants this one last big one. It'll all be over with soon."

They didn't speak much for the rest of the trip. Instead, they savored their last moments of peace and togetherness.

* * * *

When they docked, Skylar left Luke on the *Calypso*. She headed up to the main house. Her heart pounded, and she peered at bushes and trees wondering if Bill was going to jump out at her. Thankfully, she didn't encounter anyone in the entrance foyer or on the way to her room. Once inside, she hurried to the closet and pulled out her large suitcase and her carry-on. She tossed both onto the bed, and grabbed two handfuls of clothing on hangers out of the closet.

Suddenly, the door to her room opened. Lillian stood there. She smiled at Skylar. "Hello, dear. How was your day?"

"Fine," Skylar answered. Why hadn't the older woman knocked? She glanced down at the luggage on the bed and then over at Lillian. "I'm packing."

"I can see that, dear. You mustn't just stuff silk into a suitcase. You should always fold silk with tissue paper. Otherwise, you will have to get it pressed again."

"I'm in a little bit of a hurry. My ah...mentor needs me back at the college. Someone quit, and they need me to take over. I said I would come right away."

Lillian walked over to her. She picked clothing up out of the suitcase. She began to carefully refold the pieces, and then place them back in the suitcase. "How ever did your mentor manage to get a hold of you onboard the *Calypso*?" She didn't meet Skylar's gaze until she was completely finished asking the question.

Skylar wanted the plush carpet to absorb her. They both knew she had lied. "I called him from Luke's cell phone, to check in."

Lillian glanced down at a skirt in her hands. "Do you have a garment bag, dear? They're so useful for skirts and such. No? That's a pity. That was very romantic of you and Luke to go off like that. I had thought you and Martin… Well, I was confused, wasn't I?" She managed a brief, mocking laugh. "You could have confided in me. I thought you trusted me, viewed me as a friend."

"Of course I see you as a friend. I hope we can stay in touch."

"I'm afraid that won't be possible."

"Why not? Look, I didn't mean to keep you in the dark about Luke and me. I wasn't sure where we were going." Inside her head, alarms were going off. There was something definitely not right with Lillian, with the entire situation.

"I understand."

"I wasn't sure about how I felt about him, or how he felt about me," Skylar blundered on.

"Poor Martin. I'm sure he must have been disappointed. Then again, he should know by now that most young women are fickle and shallow… When I was younger, he and I were something of an item. Have I told you about how he took me to Paris. We dined at Maxim's. It was all so lovely."

Lillian was looking right at her, but her expression was distant. She was far away, lost in her memories. She shook her head, returning to the present. She placed the skirt carefully on top of the pile in the suitcase. "This is all rather unfortunate, and entirely my fault. If I had only kept a closer eye on you, some of this unpleasantness may have been avoided. Hello, Cole, Bill. We're almost ready."

Skylar glanced up. Cole stood framed in the doorway. Bill was right behind him.

"She doesn't have much, so it shouldn't take long to get her packed. I'll get her grooming accoutrements together while you gentlemen attend to the necessaries." She breezed into the bathroom without another glance at Skylar.

Shoulder to shoulder, the two men began to move in on her.

"Cole, what's going on? Did you get my note?"

"Yes, Skylar. I did. It was very thoughtful of you to fill me in on your concerns."

160

"I was all wrong…about everything. Listen to me."

But they weren't. The two men cornered her deliberately. She knew this was it, that she had to act now. She jumped up on the bed, and leaped for the doorway. Bill caught her in a flying tackle. She came down hard on her shoulder, with all of his weight driving her into the floor. He sought to pin her using his immense strength and body weight. Almost immediately, he got her arms up over her head, but she continued to inflict damage on his lower limbs. He slammed his forehead straight down onto the bridge of her nose. Her vision exploded into red shards, and then she was out.

As she came to, she experienced a moment's panic when she realized she couldn't move her hands or feet. She opened tear-filled eyes. She was lying bound on the carpet, but still in her bedroom. Cole and Bill had not yet observed that she was conscious. Wearing latex gloves, they were methodically going through all of the drawers in the dresser and in the vanity. She could hear Lillian was still at work in the bathroom.

"Do we have everything out of the closet?" Cole asked.

"I think so," Bill answered. "But it wouldn't hurt to give it the once over." He zipped her suitcase shut.

"Here's her makeup case." Lillian announced as she reappeared.

"All right. I think that's everything," Cole said. He hefted her suitcase in one hand, and her makeup bag and her carry-on in the other. "Get her on board ASAP. I should be back in a couple of hours."

"Don't screw around. The Columbians…"

"I'll be back in plenty of time." Cole cut the other man off. "I have some loose ends to tie up."

"What am I supposed to do, just carry her down?"

"That wouldn't be particularly discreet or diplomatic, especially if Luke happens to be around. He might take exception. No, use the injection. She'll walk obediently enough after that."

She began to struggle in earnest.

"You're awake." Cole hunkered down beside her. "Welcome back, Skylar. I don't think you did break her nose, Bill. It looks perfectly straight to me, albeit rather reddened."

"My aim must have been off." Bill grunted as he drained milky fluid from a small bottle into a new hypodermic needle.

"You bastard. I thought you loved Maia. I'm her sister."

"Maia," he clucked his tongue. "She was an attractive little thing. Such delicate features. So petite. I don't see any resemblance between the two of you, except for your eyes. Yes, you definitely share those, as well as an unfortunate curiosity. Your sister betrayed me, didn't you know that? She became involved with a cop, of all things. Luke was good enough to clear up that little problem for me. I'm returning the favor."

"I won't cause any problems for you. I'm leaving. There's no reason to do this."

"Yes, there is. It's all about money. It's very simple. I stand to make lots of money, and you are in the way. I can't trust you. It's time for you to disappear. Give her the sedative now, Bill."

"Please let me live. I won't tell anyone anything. I want to go home. Please. Luke will be furious if anything happens to me."

"Don't be tiresome, Skylar. You know this is the way it has to be. You are a loose end, and it's your own fault. You shouldn't have interfered. Still, I will try to ensure your demise isn't too painful." With that reassurance, he rolled her to her side.

She bit her lip against the pain of the needle plunging into her buttock. Moments later, she was hopelessly lost, mindlessly floating through an incomprehensible world.

Chapter Nineteen

She awakened to near total darkness. Her mind was still working slowly, as if through oatmeal. She turned her head, to get her face out of the pool of saliva, which had formed beneath her. She tested her body parts. Her wrists were still secured behind her, and her arms ached with pins and needles because of the enforced immobility. Her feet were also tied. Surprisingly, she was not gagged. This was probably because even if she did call out, no one in hearing distance would bother to help her.

Bill had apparently succeeded in getting her back on the *Calypso*, and they were at sea. She was lying on a bunk. She recognized that she was again in the crew's bunkroom. Down here, it was possible to feel the gentle rocking motion of the ship. In her groggy state, she found it vaguely nauseating. She considered the fact she was probably going to die. She wasn't ready to die by any means, not now when her life held so much promise. There was Luke...Where was he?

Suddenly, she was blinded with light. She closed her eyes against the painful brightness.

A hand roughly gripped her shoulder and shook her. "Come on, sleeping beauty. It's time to wake up."

Recognizing Bill's voice, and still not firing a hundred percent, she couldn't hold back the groan that escaped her lips. She was instantly furious with herself for revealing her weakness.

The man was grinning lasciviously at her. "The boss is busy, and doesn't need you yet. So there's plenty of time for us to have a little fun." He reached out and groped her breast. She twisted to get away from him, but he followed her onto the bunk. He rolled her back over and pinned her shoulder down. He cruelly pinched her nipple between his thumb and forefinger.

Unable to resist in any meaningful fashion, she spat at his face.

He grinned as he wiped her saliva off with his hairy forearm. "Yeah, fight me. It turns me on. I don't even mind that you look kind of rough. Even with the bruises, you're still hot." He peered around the small room. Two sets of narrow bunk beds were fixed to the floor on either side of it. Skylar was lying on one of the lower ones.

"Yeah, this'll work just fine." He picked her up, and dropped her unceremoniously onto the floor. He immediately straddled her. She wriggled and squirmed. He pulled out a switchblade, and sliced open the ropes tying her legs.

With her new freedom, she fought in earnest. She scissored her powerful legs about, kicking at him, but it was a losing battle. He was so much stronger, so much heavier. She fought grimly and determinedly. There was no point in screaming. No one would help her. They were at sea.

Still, her own ability to fight was the one thing she had control over. She twisted and bucked. He grabbed her by the hair, slamming the back of her head against the floor. She saw stars. She twisted her neck and sunk her teeth into the meaty flesh of his forearm.

"Son-of-a..."

The door to the tiny room opened again. "Oh dear," Lillian spoke in outraged lady-like tones. "Mr. Stevens," she remonstrated. "This is so uncivilized. What are you doing?"

"That much is obvious," Cole answered for the other man. "Let her up, Bill. Escalle needs you up top. The Columbians have raised some new issues."

"Give me ten minutes. This bitch deserves it. She bit me."

"You don't have five. You're wasting time. Get going."

Giving Cole a pissed off look, Bill released her and stood up. Skylar struggled to her feet.

"Are you all right?" Lillian asked concernedly as Bill left. She set her little handbag on the floor by the door. Then, she sought to assist Skylar by fixing her clothing.

"It doesn't really matter, does it?"

"You needn't be so hostile."

Skylar stared at the other woman in astonishment. Lillian appeared genuinely put out by her manner. She was clearly not plugged in.

"Skylar," Cole spoke as he took a seat on one of the bunks. "Nothing is written in stone. It would be to your advantage to speak frankly with me."

"You mean you won't kill me? I find that highly unlikely."

"I'm not a crude, brutal character like Bill. You trusted me once. It could benefit you to do so again. Who are you working for?"

"I don't work for anyone."

"FBI, ATF, Homeland Security?"

"Cole, you know I came to Casa del Mar to find out what happened to my sister. That's all there is to it. I'm a complete amateur. That should be obvious by now."

"You have been in contact with someone."

"Skylar dear, you really should tell him everything." Lillian offered, as she fluttered back toward the door. "Cole is a very clever fellow."

"There's nothing to tell. I should have gone to someone, but I didn't. I was stupid."

"The only person with whom you've had any discussions regarding Casa del Mar and its occupants was your friend?"

Oh God. Laura. What had she done to her? "She doesn't know anything. Honestly. I don't know anything, for that matter."

"How long have you known Luke is a cop?"

Suddenly, she realized what the conversation was really about. Cole was after bigger game. "He works for Mr. Escalle."

"There's no point in protecting him. I already know everything. He's FBI, isn't he?"

Obviously, he didn't know 'everything', or he wouldn't be asking her these questions. She focused her heart and her mind on the thought of Luke. If she could protect him, then her death would have some meaning.

"Come on, Cole," she mocked. "Does he seem like secret agent material? I'll admit he's good looking, charming, very talented in bed, but he's completely without morals. He's the perfect whore. Luke will be loyal to your boss for as long as it's profitable for him."

He assessed her with his eyes. "So you wouldn't be upset if he took a swimming lesson today?"

"I think it would be a waste of some real talent, but go right ahead. I don't owe Luke anything. We had a good time. That's it."

"You surprise me. I hadn't thought you were so cold, so jaded. You've given me some food for thought." He rose to his feet. "Now, if you ladies will excuse me, I'm going to have a word with Martin. Lillian?"

"I'll just stay here and keep Skylar company."

"All right. If that's what you want to do. Skylar, don't bother trying to overpower Lillian here. We have eight men on board, one posted right outside your door. You won't get far."

She swallowed hard as the door closed. Ignoring the other woman, she sat back down on a bunk. Then, she heard an ominous, metallic click.

Lillian was twisting a black cylinder onto the end of a slim, elegant derringer. Her purse lay opened at her feet.

"Skylar, I don't approve of violence, but I'm afraid you have given me no alternatives. I thought you were different from that slut Yvette and the others, but you are all the same, all after poor Martin. I am so disappointed in you, and I can't allow you to cause any more problems."

"What are you doing?"

"Now, if you will only sit still. This shouldn't hurt." She took a step closer.

"Lillian, I have never had any interest in Mr. Escalle. I came here for information about my sister, Maia." She repeated the now familiar litany.

"Why couldn't you just leave? Yvette made the same mistake after she embarrassed Martin so terribly at that party. That girl was so ungrateful. The next morning, I went to help her with her packing. She refused to get out of bed. She said she was going to make Martin pay, that he was going to have to drag her out of the house.

"I couldn't allow her to upset him again. So I offered to bring her some of my sweet tea for her headache. It was so simple really to dissolve her sleeping pills into the tea. She even asked me to hand her some. I just dumped the rest right in. She was so out of it, she never even noticed. Those police officers were so nice and understanding about it all.

"Did you know that girl had tried to commit suicide several times before? I don't think she was ever serious about it. I think she made the threats to get attention. Those attempts certainly enhanced the believability of my story. All right now, there's not much time. I would appreciate if you would take the blanket off of that cot and lay it on the floor."

"Lillian, my hands."

"Oh yes. I see. Well, just drop it down. That will have to do. Now you lie down right there. Put your head on the blanket. This way, we won't get a big mess everywhere. I'll be able to scoop all of it up in the blanket, and throw it overboard. That will be so much tidier."

Skylar obediently picked up the blanket. But, now she realized the 'it' the other woman was referring to was her brains. She froze. "Lillian, I don't want Martin Escalle. Contrary to what Cole says, I'm no threat to anyone. Please help me. I'll leave, and you'll never hear from me again."

"You are a disappointment. I believed you were an honest person. You may not be interested in Martin in the romantic sense, but you are after him. You want to get him into trouble, and I can't allow that to happen. Now, please lie down."

"No way. I'm not going to make this easy for you. You're insane."

Lillian pursed her lips, clearly distraught about her lack of cooperation. "It would probably be less painful for you if you would be still. I'm not that good a shot. You don't want to draw this out. I need to be finished before Cole returns. He might interfere." She raised her derringer, taking aim.

Skylar ducked and dodged like a prizefighter, trying to make as challenging a target as possible. "Oh God! Oh God... *Please*."

A gun went off, reverberating through the small room. Blood and human matter splattered her face and clothing.

But she was still standing.

Chapter Twenty

Skylar watched as Lillian collapsed to the floor, her face completely gone. Skylar glanced up in disbelief to see Cole standing there, a gun gripped in his hand.

"That's unfortunate," he commented as he stepped over Lillian's body. "She was loyal, but she was becoming a liability. She's always been completely obsessed with Martin, but she was coming unhinged. I told Martin he should encourage her to take an early retirement. She wouldn't hear of it. It was only a matter of time before something like this happened."

"She was going to kill me."

"Yes, she was. That would have been an unfortunate development at this point. We need your assistance in a matter. You're a mess." He stepped closer to her, and she retreated, but there was nowhere to go. "Hold still," he ordered, pulling a switchblade out of his pocket. He reached around behind her, and slit the rope binding her hands. "Here," he added and tossed a blanket to her.

She caught it awkwardly with hands that were stiff and painful.

"Wipe yourself off and follow me."

A shiver went down her spine as she stepped over Lillian's body. "You're just going to leave her here?"

"I'll send someone down to clean up. Go on ahead of me."

With a gun at her back, following Cole's directions, she proceeded up to the deck. The night sky was dark velvet pierced with silver pinpricks. The fresh breeze stripped away the last of her drug-induced fogginess. As she was still only wearing a tank top and shorts, she was cold.

Martin, Bill, Angelique, and Luke were already assembled there, as

168

were two bodyguard-looking types whom she didn't recognize. Angelique was standing with her back to the others, staring out over the obsidian waves. Luke and Bill were seated in a semicircle facing Martin.

Luke met her glance, but his eyes were shuttered and distant. Almost immediately, he looked away.

She had to trust him. He wasn't coming over to her because of the heavily armed goons. She was sure she had never seen these guys before. Maybe they came from the Columbians. Clearly, something big was impending.

"So good of you to join us, Ms. Connelly. I find I need your help. I've arrived at a critical juncture in my endeavors and I must ascertain the absolute loyalty of my comrades. To that end, I've gathered my little team together here. You see, I'm planning to leave the U.S. in due course, but I must remain for several more months and wind up my business interests…"

"When you leave, I am not going with you." Angelique shouted, spinning away from her position by the rail. Her thick, dark hair blew wild and loose, partially obscuring her face. "Martin, you cannot make me go."

"Of course, I can," he answered mildly. "You are my only sister. You will go with me wherever I choose. Your son's continued safety depends upon your cooperation."

"You wouldn't harm your own nephew." She fairly spat the words out.

"Are you completely sure of that?" He responded, pressing his fingertips together to form an arch. "I never wanted you to marry that bastard, Whitfield. I warned you against it. The child is of tainted blood. I've only tolerated him to this point because of you."

"Chris is your nephew. You couldn't…My God, you are a monster! Jim was right about you."

"Compose yourself. You are distraught. Cole will escort you to your stateroom. Do be so kind as to take something to soothe your nerves."

"I'm not going along with this. I will not cooperate."

"You will if you want your son to live. I had no problem killing the father. I can assure you disposing of the boy will pose me little difficulty."

Angelique broke down into sobs. Cole led the devastated woman away.

Skylar felt sorry for her. Martin's sister was well and truly trapped, but at least she and her son would live. In that, there was some hope.

"Now," Martin checked his watch, "we don't have much time, and I have an issue that needs to be resolved immediately. Luke, Bill, I know one of you has been ripping me off. I've known for months. It didn't really bother me, because only insignificant amounts were involved. However, now I learn that one of my team has been attempting to get into contact with the Columbians, trying to cut me out. I cannot tolerate that kind of disloyalty."

"How do you know Cole isn't the crook?" Bill demanded, his tone, brisk and irritated. Tense anger radiated from the man.

"I have known Cole Hollins for ten years. He has proven his loyalty to me many times. He is my right hand, as well as my eyes and ears. He would never betray me, but I have grave reservations about the two of you. I have devised a little test."

Luke said nothing. He simply sat there, taking it in.

"Luke, shall we start with you? You are familiar with Ms. Connelly." His tone was light but sarcastic.

One of the goons gripped her right hand, pushed it high up her back, and shoved her forward. She bit her cheek against the pain, but refused to cry out. She knew she was soon going to die. There was no point in pretending otherwise, but she wouldn't behave in a cowardly fashion. She didn't intend to ruin Luke's investigation now, at the very end. Too many people had been hurt or killed, Maia, Angelique and her husband, Chris, and Yvette. She accepted the price of justice for all of them might very well be her own life.

"Skylar?" Martin rose from his seat. He strolled around somewhere behind her. "By now, we are all aware you came here looking for information about your sister, Maia, whom Luke here dispatched. Whom have you spoken with?"

"I already told Cole, I don't work for anyone and I haven't spoken to anyone. I came to the Keys looking for information about Maia's disappearance, but I haven't been able to come up with anything substantial."

"Do you really expect me to believe that?"

"I only spoke to the police after I was shot at in Key West."

"That was clumsily done, Bill." Martin remonstrated.

"I didn't want to kill her, just to scare her away. I knew she was a nosey bitch after I found her snooping around your office. It's because I'm loyal to you I took those shots at her."

"Yes, and drew more attention to me and to my home. You are reckless, Bill, and often impetuous. That aspect of your nature could prove troublesome to me in the future."

"You're here to clean house," Luke remarked coolly.

"That's correct, Luke. I want everything in order before I embark on my new life. The Columbians will not tolerate any sort of disorder in their business partners' affairs. So, back to Ms. Connelly." He stepped into her line of vision. "The time for games is over. Who are you working for?"

"Do you really think some agency would send me here to look for my sister? I'm not an agent. I have no training. I didn't tell you Maia and I were sisters, but you could have found that out easily enough. We have different last names, but that was no big secret. Still, you hired me and I came. I only wanted to find out what happened to Maia. It's the truth."

"Actually, I do believe you, but what about your relationship with Luke here? Men are notoriously indiscreet after a sexual encounter. Did he share any information with you?"

"Give me a break, Martin. I'm not some kid who got laid for the first time. I found her hiding on the *Calypso*, and I got my rocks off," he said and shrugged nonchalantly. "She's no Mata Hari."

She stared at Luke in anguished horror. He couldn't mean it. He had to be playing a role. Still, she had never seen any proof he was ATF.

No. She couldn't allow herself to think this way. She had to trust him.

"She does have a lean, fit sort of appeal." Martin remarked as he tipped her chin up with his fingertips.

She sought to turn her head away, but found her neck squeezed in a vice-like grip by the unknown man standing behind her.

"Well, Luke, if she has only been a recreational activity for you, you won't mind if we dispose of her." Martin turned away.

171

Chapter Twenty-One

Skylar saw a muscle clench in Luke's jaw.

"Kill the bitch," Bill eagerly seconded. "The Columbians will be here soon, so let's get it over with. I'll even do the honors." He reached under his sports jacket to his shoulder holster, and pulled his weapon out.

And the night exploded with sound and fury.

Skylar squeezed her eyes closed. She opened them in time to watch Bill Stevens collapse to the deck. His expression of complete surprise and utter disbelief would be forever etched in her memory. A pool of blood oozed out from under him.

Cole stood framed by the doorway, which led into the salon. He held a gun in his hand. He killed Bill. "He was a fool, Martin." He offered in explanation. "A liability to you, to all of us."

"I appreciate your concern, Cole, but I wanted to handle the situation in my own way. You killed him too quickly. I planned to gather some information from him." Escalle's tone was mildly rebuking, but the look in his eyes was intense and furious. "Give me your gun, Cole. I will not tolerate any more 'accidents'.

Martin rattled something off in rapid Spanish to the two goons. They immediately picked up Bill's body and hefted it overboard with utter nonchalance.

Skylar felt an icy shiver travel its way up her spine. Was she soon to join Bill?

"I thought you trusted me, Martin," Cole rebuked.

"The gun, Cole."

Cole and Martin faced each other silently. There was something significant and dangerous passing between them. Cole eventually yielded.

He looked down, then extended his weapon to the older man.

Martin took it and carefully set it down on the glass-topped table. "Take a seat, Cole."

He silently obeyed.

"Now, back to our star-crossed lovers. Skylar, you have attempted to deceive me from the first. Your usefulness to me is at an end. Luke, you are another story. I would like to trust you, to include you in my future endeavors. You have some very valuable skills. I know that you, unlike the unfortunate Mr. Stevens, are a man of honor and of values. He was a crook, but that matter is now finished. You do not kill hastily or easily," this mild rebuke was directed at Cole. "I need you to prove yourself to me. I have devised a simple test for you. Kill Skylar, and I will know you are my man. Fail to do so, and I will have you both killed."

Luke didn't flinch. He met the other man's gaze. "How will killing her prove my loyalty to you? All it will demonstrate is that I value my own life over hers. Surely, you don't doubt that fact?"

"Oh, but I do, Luke. Skylar Connelly will die today whether or not you pull the trigger, but I want you to do it."

"Why?"

"Because I know killing her will not be easy for you. It will prove to me I own you, you will obey me even if you disagree with my directives."

"The woman is foolish but not dangerous."

"Your sympathy for her is touching, but she took the risk by coming to Casa del Mar. Potentially, if she lives, she could prove very dangerous, indeed. She now knows too much. No, my decision is made. Here take this gun." He slid the weapon across the smooth table to Luke, who picked it up automatically. "Do it, Luke. Don't throw yourself away on a woman. You had no problem killing the sister. With me, you'll soon have enough money to buy as many women as you want, younger and prettier ones."

Luke stood up unhurriedly. He pivoted and faced her. He raised the gun ever so slowly until his arm was extended, the barrel of the pistol, targeted on her heart.

In that moment, she knew there were worse ways to die. At least, it would be quick. She would go with the satisfaction of knowing she protected her sister and Luke. He had to kill her, she told herself, to save the mission.

Then, he winked at her. Her heart soared. He had a plan.

"Let her go." He ordered to the goon holding her. The man obeyed the nod from Martin, and she nearly slumped to the ground when his support was gone. She struggled to stay up, and she faced Luke.

"Step back," he directed.

"What?"

"Just do it. Step back."

She did so. They were engaged in a very slow, hesitant sort of dance. He would advance a step, and she would fall back. She stopped when she felt the deck rail against the small of her back.

"Very thoughtful of you, Luke. By killing her over there, we won't have so much of a mess on the deck."

Skylar never thought Lillian and Escalle had much in common. So it was rather absurdly peculiar to her they shared this concern over how 'messy' killing her could be.

At the sound of Martin's voice, they both froze in their respective positions. Their eyes met. It was then she became aware of the music drifting up from one of the staterooms below. She recognized the tune. It was by the Wiggles, an Australian foursome, which performed kid music in brightly colored shirts of various shades. Chris had several Wiggles videos, and Skylar watched them with him on more than one occasion. Apparently, he was viewing one of them right now. How bizarre, she reflected. She was going to die with the Wiggles echoing through her mind.

"Just get it over with," she whispered frantically to Luke. Why was he drawing this out?

He glanced down at the rail and then back up at her. As she watched, he did it again, very deliberately.

"Hurry up, Luke," Cole directed. "We're running out of time."

She realized he wanted her to go over the side, to jump into the black waves that lapped at the *Calypso*. She had no idea how far away the land was, but in the distance, she could see some faint yellow lights. He was giving her a fighting chance.

Skylar stared at him, taking all of him in. She sought to etch this image of him into her memory, because it was unlikely both of them would survive the night.

She counted slowly, mouthing the words. He nodded at two. Just as she was about to get to three, the door to the salon swung wide. Chris charged into the fray. He was crying and wild and he threw himself on his uncle. Escalle was taken by surprise. His chair went over, and he fell to the deck grappling with the boy.

Angelique was right behind her son. She hurled herself atop her brother, attempting to aid or protect Chris.

"You won't kill Skylar the way you did Dad. You won't! I won't let you!"

Skylar recognized her opportunity, and took it. She dove over the rail. The air rushed by her cool and salty, and then she plunged into the warmer water. Disoriented, she sought to surface and clunked her head on something hard and flat. She pushed off, and swam strongly away from the hull of the *Calypso*.

God, please take care of Luke, and of Chris, too. Please.

She started to stroke deliberately, the setting and the intent felt very familiar after her adventures of the day before. The powerful muscles of her legs and shoulders worked automatically, elegantly. She couldn't let herself think about the fathoms beneath her that swarmed with aquatic life. Nor could she allow worry about Luke to weaken her. She had to carry on, for him, to make sure Martin Escalle faced justice eventually.

Twenty minutes later, she was so caught up in her rhythm that the helicopter was nearly over her head before she heard it. She paused, glancing back. Two well lit boats were moving in on the still *Calypso*. The Columbians were arriving in style.

Beams of light originating from the brightly lit helicopter searched the water. In no time at all, one was trained upon her. She treaded water as the helicopter came closer. It was over her head now. Escape seemed impossible. It came lower and lower still, stirring up the water around her.

She watched as its door opened. She waited for the inevitable sharp shooter to appear. Instead, to her amazement, the man poised there tossed an inflatable yellow raft out. It hit the water not far from her.

A voice boomed out over the water: "Ma'am, please swim to the raft. We'll get someone down there to help you A.S.A.P."

She waved euphorically as she read: *United States Coast Guard* on the side of the helicopter.

Chapter Twenty-Two

It was already well into another golden afternoon before Skylar emerged from the Spanish-style stucco building that housed the Key West branch of the Bureau of Customs and Border Protection. She was thoroughly worn out and famished. Since her arrival late the night before, she had consumed only a day-old donut, convenience machine pretzels, and some rather rank coffee. She was relieved when Special Agent Jake Dorrance ordered fast food for her from a drive-through on their way to a nearby motel.

She made quick work of the hot roast beef, curly fries, and milk shake. It all tasted divine. There was nothing like a thousand calories of fat and sugar to pick one up. Still, she couldn't stop worrying about Luke, hoping he was all right and she would see him soon.

By the time they had arrived at the motel, and secured her room, the sustenance revived her. She wanted to talk. She had been plied with questions on and off for ten hours. Now, she wanted some answers.

"I can't believe it's all over," she commented as she slid her key card into the lock. Jake was younger than she was, about her height, and seemed a nice guy. She felt comfortable around him.

"Yeah, I know. It's kind of a strange feeling. This investigation has been going on for a long time."

"I'll be able to leave Key West soon?"

"That's what the boss said. Tomorrow we'll need you to verify some details, and look at some pictures. Then, you're free to go. If we need anything else, we'll get in touch with you. That's it, until the trial. You'll probably have to come back for that."

"No problem. Anything I can do to help."

"I should get going."

"Not yet. I just want to know… One of the agents, a big man with a moustache?"

"You mean Walters?"

"Yes. He told me Luke is all right, but he wouldn't tell me anything else. Why wasn't Luke at the station? Where did he go?"

He shifted his weight, and glanced down at his feet. "I'm not supposed to discuss his condition with a non-family member."

Her heart racing, she decided to bluff him. "Luke and I…we're planning on getting married. So you see, I'm almost family."

Surprise dawned on Jake's very likeable features. He grinned, appearing more like a very fit college jock than an investigative agent. "You and Luke are planning on getting hitched. I'll be damned. That's great."

"Please tell me what happened on board the *Calypso*. I won't be able to sleep until I know."

He considered for a moment. Then, he nodded. "All right. It's over with now, so I don't see any harm. Can I come in?" He followed her into the small, generic motel bedroom done in pastel shades of pink and green. They sat down on the jungle patterned vinyl chairs that flanked a small, circular table.

"You went over the side when the boy, Christopher, ran out and attacked his uncle. Turns out the kid witnessed his father's execution. It really screwed him up. That scumbag completely intimidated Christopher so he kept his mouth shut, and didn't even tell his mother."

"Chris was only four or five when his father…"

"I know, but he witnessed it. Because the kid knew what happened, Escalle worked to keep the boy and his mother separated. The kid never breathed a word about what happened with his father until last night. Apparently, seeing his mother angry and hysterical got to him. He lost it. He attacked his uncle. In the confusion, Luke took out the bodyguards."

"You mean, he killed them?" The thought of Luke killing another human being was chilling to Skylar, even if that person was a 'bad guy'.

"Luke, no way," Jake chuckled. "He knocked one guy out, and wounded the other. He's so good sometimes, it's scary." The young agent didn't bother to mask his admiration for the other man. "While Luke was screwing around with the bodyguards, Cole came at him with a knife. Luke got cut pretty badly. Don't worry," he raised his hands here. "It wasn't life threatening or anything. By the time we got on board, he had all four of them contained. He was sitting there on a lounge chair with his gun trained on them, holding a bloody towel to his leg. He was like Clint Eastwood… Anyway, you didn't see him afterwards because he went to the hospital right away to get patched up. The guy may get a commendation for this investigation, but I don't envy him the paperwork."

Blowing out a deep breath, she sat back. For the first time in days, she felt she could breathe easily. "When can I see him?"

"I can't answer that one." He glanced down at his wristwatch. "Aw shit, I gotta go. I gotta pick up some VIPS in Miami. It's one of the joys of being one of the younger guys." He offered her a quick grin and then was gone.

For the first few hours, Skylar found it nearly impossible to relax. Her mind was spinning. She took a shower and flipped aimlessly through TV stations. She was debating heading out and hitting a gas station for some ice cream. Then, the phone rang. Thinking it might be Luke, she grabbed it on the second ring.

"Hello? Yes, this is Skylar Connelly. No, I don't need anything. I thought I would step out for a minute… Okay, I'll stay in my room… I understand. All right. Tomorrow morning at eight. I'll be ready. Good night…Oh. Wait, is it okay if I call my mother and let her know what's going on? Thanks. Bye."

Looking forward to a good, cathartic talk with her mom, she dialed the digits. Unfortunately, after four rings, her mother's answering machine picked up. She left her phone number and room number, then hung up. Skylar lay back in the bed, with her arms behind her head, and stared up at the ceiling. Then, she glanced over at the nightstand table. Just seven-thirty. What was she going to do until morning?

She reached again for the remote control and flipped channels. At some point, she must have dozed off. The sound of a firm knock on the door awoke her abruptly. She glanced over and saw it was now one o'clock. Who would be coming to her room at this time of night?

She had the immediate and paranoid thought one of Escalle's cronies had discovered her location and was now after her. There was no way out of the room except through the door or the window beside it. She was well and truly trapped, and completely alone. Why hadn't they assigned an agent to protect her?

There was another knock on the door. This time, louder and more insistent. She looked around for her purse, and glimpsed it kicked under the small table right by the door. She dived for it, and dumped it out on her bed. Frantically, she tossed aside her checkbook, her daily minder, and a tube of lip-gloss. Where was the mace?

Not that it would do her any good if they came in shooting. There was no time. She heard a soft scraping sound, and then the doorknob turned. The door swung open, and she dove down beside the bed. Closing her eyes, she waited for the guns to start firing.

"Are you sure we have the right room?" An-oh-so-familiar female voice demanded. "There's no one in here. The woman at the desk must have given you the wrong room number."

Was it possible? After all this time? Skylar rose to a kneeling position.

"Skylar? What are you doing down there?" The woman before her sported a jagged pixie-cut in an unnaturally white shade. She was angular and extremely thin, but the misty green eyes now filling with tears were without a doubt her sister's.

"Maia." She whispered the name. She was unaware she had risen to her feet. The two women stared at each other. Skylar grabbed her and hugged her close. Both were sobbing openly and laughing when they finally broke apart. "You look so different. Are you okay?"

A man cleared his throat by the door. Skylar glanced over and saw Luke standing there. "Luke, you're here."

"That's a pretty lame 'Hello.' I was hoping for some more enthusiasm."

She didn't need any more encouragement. She launched herself at him. He caught her, absorbing the impact of her body striking his. He grunted in reaction.

"You're hurt. I'm sorry. Where? Is it bad?"

"Cole got me through the thigh." Luke's lips were thinned with pain. "He didn't hit anything vital. I'll be fine. The doctors at the hospital said I was good to go. I wanted to be here sooner, but I had to finish up some things at the station. When I heard Jake was on his way back to town with Maia here, I thought I'd join the party."

"I'm really glad you did, but are you sure you're all right?"

"Really, Skylar. It's not a big deal. I had a few stitches, a tetanus booster, and some antibiotics. I'm as good as new."

"Don't you two sound all cozy and domestic," Maia observed, grinning at them. "So, do I hear wedding bells?"

"Maia." Skylar shook her head, her eyes on Luke.

"Look, there's nothing like coming back from the dead to focus you."

"We haven't even talked about…"

"Haven't we?" Luke asked, his tone, suddenly serious. He reached out and took her hands in his. "I know that it's too soon to ask you anything. This has been a very unnatural situation, and I should wait until things settle down, but I'm afraid that if I don't say something now, you'll walk right out of my life. Before I leave you ladies alone tonight, I'd like to know what your plans are."

"I don't have to get back for a few more weeks."

"You two are the worst," Maia observed. "It's obvious both of you are too chicken to say how you really feel. So if you don't mind, I'm going out to the car for a minute to grab my bag and to talk to Jake. He and I have a lot of catching up to do. You two have ten minutes, then I'm coming back."

"You don't have to go, Maia. We're…"

Maia held up her hand, stopping her sister. "I said ten minutes. Starting now." She strode confidently from the room. The gentle saunter that had once characterized her movement was now wholly gone.

"She's changed," Skylar commented.

"Bar tending in New Jersey will do that for you," he observed with a familiar cock to his eyebrow. "She's right, you know. I may not be the most poetic guy, but I…care about you. I want us to be together. If you want to head back up north, I can transfer to a different office somewhere up there. I don't want 'us' to be over now. Look Skylar, I know that there's something special between us. I love—" He hesitated, taking a breath.

"I'm not trying to rush you into anything. We need time, normal time with nothing dramatic going on, to get to know each other better. That's all I'm asking for."

She stopped him by placing a finger to his lips. "That's exactly what I wanted to hear." She gripped him by the front of his shirt and pulled him to her. "I love you," she murmured against his lips.

"I love you, too."

Epilogue

Several months after she'd left Key West, Skylar got a letter from Chris, in which he related that he'd swum well at a YMCA meet. She smiled as she read it. She was proud of the boy, who'd been through so much, yet seemed to be putting the past and his fears behind him.

The wheels of justice turned slowly, she mused, tapping the envelope against her palm. It had taken more than a year to prepare the State's case against Martin Escalle. His attorneys requested and were granted a change of venue as the Judge didn't feel that Escalle could get a fair trial in a county where he was so well known. In the end, he was convicted of arms trafficking and sentenced to fifteen years in prison. In addition, he was charged in the murder of his brother-in-law, Jim Whitfield. His trial on that charge was still pending.

Cole Hollins was also facing significant charges and was attempting to make a deal with prosecutors by becoming a witness for the State against his former boss. Regardless, both men could look forward to spending a significant portion of their futures behind bars.

Maia went back to school and finished her education degree, then she'd headed back to the Keys. She was teaching at an elementary school on Key Largo. When Maia came home for Christmas, Jake Dorrance in tow, both Skylar and her mother found they liked Maia's young man.

Skylar smiled. Her mother even approved of Luke, not that her objections would have mattered. They knew they wanted to be together, they were right for each other. Even though, for some time, the details of life intruded while Luke was concluding his investigation, and she was completing her Master's. Afterward, they'd taken three months and cruised to the Caribbean and back up the East Coast on his sailboat.

Now, she stood in the small bedroom of her apartment, packing for her honeymoon.

"What are you thinking?" Luke put his arms around her and pulled her back against him.

"That I can't believe we're here, together, after all we've been through, that we're actually getting married today."

"Honey, the greatest adventure of our lives is just about to begin."

"I'm ready for anything as long as I'm with you."

About the Author

Isabelle Kane believes that romance and love are among the most delightful aspects of the human experience. She seeks to provide her readers with rich tapestries of stories in which love is just one element of the forces that intertwine the lives of her protagonists. She believes every dreamer deserves the adventures and escape offered by an exciting novel. The greatest sources of joy and inspiration in Isabelle's life are her husband and their three children. Isabelle is a graduate of Bryn Mawr College and holds an MA in English from the University of Wisconsin-Eau Claire.

www.kaneandtremaine.com

Other Works by the Author with Melange Books, LLC
Satin Romance Imprint

One Last Farewell